Life of Sin 3

Lock Down Publications and Ca$h Presents

Life of Sin 3

A Novel by *T.J. & Jelissa*

Life of Sin 3

Lock Down Publications
P.O. Box 870494
Mesquite, Tx 75187

Visit our website @
www.lockdownpublications.com

Copyright 2019 by T.J. & Jelissa
Life of Sin 3

Lock Down Publications
Like our page on Facebook: Lock Down Publications @
www.facebook.com/lockdownpublications.ldp
Cover design and layout by: **Dynasty Cover Me**
Book interior design by: **Shawn Walker**
Edited by: **Kierra Northington**

Stay Connected with Us!

Text **LOCKDOWN** to 22828 to stay up-to-date with new releases, sneak peaks, contests and more…

Thank you.

Submission Guideline.

Submit the first three chapters of your completed manuscript to ldpsubmissions@gmail.com, subject line: Your book's title. The manuscript must be in a .doc file and sent as an attachment. Document should be in Times New Roman, double spaced and in size 12 font. Also, provide your synopsis and full contact information. If sending multiple submissions, they must each be in a separate email.

Have a story but no way to send it electronically? You can still submit to LDP/Ca$h Presents. Send in the first three chapters, written or typed, of your completed manuscript to:

LDP: Submissions Dept
Po Box 870494
Mesquite, Tx 75187

DO NOT send original manuscript. Must be a duplicate.

Provide your synopsis and a cover letter containing your full contact information.

Thanks for considering LDP and Ca$h Presents.

T.J. & Jelissa

Chapter 1
Bentley

Time was ticking; my heart was pounding in my chest. One last move and it was all over. We'd be scot-free to start a new life outside the country. The only person standing in the way. Blanco. As long as he had breath in his body, our lives could not go back to normal. He had to be dealt with accordingly.

I watched from a distance, as he wrapped his arm around a petite Spanish female. She whispered something in his ear that made him hold up one finger. A big dude walked over to him and whispered something in his other ear. This made him perk up. He scanned the expanse of the party, and his eyes seemed to stop on me and Jade, or maybe I was tripping. Then, he continued to look over the people in the party, before the big goon walked away nodding his head. The Spanish female rubbed his chest and pulled him down so she could whisper into his ear again. Whatever she said to him caused him to laugh. He looked behind her and ran his hand over her ass. Squeezed it and sucked his bottom lip. She took his hand and led him through the party. They made their way toward the stairs, right before the same big goon from a few seconds ago jogged to him and whispered into his ear.

This made him perk up. He frowned and shook off the Spanish chick just as the waiters came through, pushing carts filled with silver platters of all kinds of powders. Blanco headed to the front of the mansion and out of sight. The Spanish chick stood with her arms crossed, took out her phone and began to text on it like crazy.

Jade rubbernecked, watching the event unfold just as I was. "Baby, something ain't right. I don't know what's going on, but something is most definitely wrong."

I felt the heavy pistol tucked in my waistband. I didn't know what was going on either, but as long as I was strapped I felt like I was prepared for it. "Yeah, boo, you're right. Come on. Let's blend into this party a lil bit. We down to seven minutes before we gotta go kamikaze and smoke that nigga. Either way, he gotta inhale these slugs. He the only one standing in the way of our new life. Fuck that." I was getting more and more irritated by the second. I wanted to be done. Gone and on the highway already, headed toward the border.

Jade took my hand and we wound up on the dance floor, grooving to a song by Alicia Keys. We danced about and got closer and closer to the area of where Blanco had disappeared. Once we were close enough, I was able to look down the hallway to see him and the big goon still locked in a deep conversation. Blanco's arms swung wildly through the air as he chewed the dude out. Then, he was storming down the hallway, angry and taking big steps. I searched for the two men from earlier that acted as security for him. They were nowhere in sight.

"Baby, he coming this way. What do we do?" Jade asked, tensing up.

"Nothin, just keep dancing. We're good." I grabbed her soft ass, kneading it like dough. Man, Jade's body was amazing. I couldn't get over how perfect it was to me, and I knew the baby would only add to her bodily perfection. I couldn't wait. The lust in me nearly caused me to lose my focus. I glanced at my watch and saw we literally had only a few minutes until his crew from South America was set to show up.

The Spanish chick from earlier came and stepped in front of him. Ran her fingers through her long hair and started to say something, before running her hands over his chest.

Blanco hugged her to him and palmed her ass, much like I'd done Jade's. Whispered into her ear and laughed, as he nodded his head toward the stairs.

She licked her juicy, red-coated lips, and pulled him toward them. They made their way up the stairs and I felt a sense of relief.

"That must be the chick the sista was telling me about. She said he would lead her up the stairs. Let's wait a minute, then we gon follow them," Jade said, mugging the pair. She looked so fuckin' sexy looking all evil and shit.

"Fuck that. We gotta go hit dude ass now." I looked toward the front door as a group of Spanish men eased into the party. They were tatted up all over their faces and necks. Instead of being casually dressed like everybody else, they wore plaid shirts and khaki pants. I saw this after they took their coats off and handed them to the help.

Jade's eyes got bucked as she looked them over. "Damn. They definitely look like they about that life. They waist look chunky too, baby. They must not have gone through the metal detector."

I peeped the same thing. Took her hand and headed toward the steps. "Come on."

We took them swiftly. Got to the top of the flight and heard the sounds of loud moaning already. "Damn, he ain't waste no time, did he?" I asked, looking down to Jade.

"He probably knew them dudes were on the way. Tryna hurry up and get him a quickie." She slid the gun out of her bag and cocked it like I'd shown her.

I put some pep in my step. Rushed down the hallway and stopped at the room I knew the pair must have been in. Looked Jade over and took the nine out of my waistband. Counting with my fingers, I held up one, then two of them, and then the third. Turned the knob and pushed the door inward.

Blanco had the Spanish girl bent over the oak desk, fucking her hard from the back with his pants around his ankles. His eyes were closed and he was breathing harder than a dog pulling a sled. When the Spanish female saw us, she screamed, "Just him, not me."

Blanco's eyes shot open. He frowned. "What are you doing up here, chico? The party is downstairs."

"Hurry, baby," Jade urged.

I raised the gun and fired four quick shots. *Zoop. Zoop. Zoop. Zoop.* The firearm jumped in my hand. Big sparks flew out of it, despite the silencer on the end of it. The room filled with the stench of burnt gunpowder.

Blanco flew over the desk and wound up on his back, bloodied. He struggled to get up, breathing heavy, cursing in Spanish. I rushed over to him and put three more into him at point-blank range, deading him. He lay in the middle of the floor, a big puddle of blood forming around his body.

The Spanish woman covered her head. I stopped in front of her ready to blast, when Jade grabbed my wrist. "Nall, baby. We're done now. Let's get the heck out of here. Give her a pass."

I mugged the broad and everything in my soul told me to ice her as well. But instead, I listened to my rib and we jetted out of there. Hopped in the whip and stormed away from the scene before anybody became the wiser.

***

The next morning, I met up with Guns at a burger spot on 33rd Street in South Camden. He slid into the back of the whip and started up right away. "Nigga, yousa monster. Both of y'all. Damn, y'all handled ya bidness, and wit all of them Brazilian niggas there too. Y'all the truth, man. Word to my mother, y'all the truth." He handed me a small Crown Royal knapsack. "It got everything in there. The IDs, the social security cards. The passports. Yo, y'all have a nice life. Word up. Get the fuck off of the East Coast at the very least."

I turned around and smiled at him. "Yo, good looking, bruh. My word, you looked out. I owe you, kid, if there is ever anything I can do for you once I settle, just let me know."

Jade turned and adjusted herself in her seat. Then, she began to rifle through the Gucci bag the dark-skinned sista had given her, as if she'd lost something.

Guns laughed. "It's all good. But, bruh, you know they already putting up a half-million dollars on the heads of the mafuckas that kilt Blanco. That's crazy, ain't it? I mean, that shit just happened yesterday." He laughed again and looked out of the back window, then back up to me.

"He must of been a major nigga, that's all," I said out loud. "Yo, but anyway, we about to embark on this journey, bruh, I'ma fuck wit you in a minute." I turned around and started the car.

Guns nodded and with lightning speed, upped a .40 Glock out of his waistband and slammed it into the back of my head so hard I could feel it bust my skull. "Niggas, they want that ass dead or alive, and I ain't passing up on no half million dollars for nobody. Not even for my dope feen ass mother. Ain't nothing personal. Forgive me, Dunn."

Boom. Boom. Boom. Boom.

T.J. & Jelissa

Chapter 2
Bentley

Boom. Boom. Boom. Boom.

I covered my head off of instinct, as the scent of gunpowder and burnt leather wafted into my nostrils. By the time I looked up, Jade was kneeling in her passenger's seat with her gun smoking.

Boom. Boom.

"I knew we couldn't trust you, Guns. I just knew it!" she screamed, her face balled into a scowl.

Guns lay against the back seat with his eyes wide open, with holes in his face and neck. Blood poured out of each one, before he slid to his left. His head wound up against the window, tongue hanging out of his mouth.

I glanced over to Jade. She breathed heavy, before replacing the gun into her Gucci bag. "Damn. I'm tired of the killing, Bentley. I'm tired of the killing, but he was gon shoot you, baby. He was finna kill you just like Santana was. Look, he put two bullets in the roof." She pointed toward the ceiling of the car.

Sure enough, there were two big holes there. I guessed Jade's bullets had caught him off guard. As hers was hitting him, his finger had pulled on his trigger twice, thereby letting loose and sending the slugs flying into the car's ceiling. I honestly believed had Jade not done that, I would have been a dead man.

"Baby. Damn. Baby." I grabbed her to me. Held her in my arms and relished in the fact that she was my rib, my rider. That she would buss that gun for me against all odds. Jade had saved my life twice. "I love you so much, boo. Thank you. You're my everything, boo. I mean that shit."

"I love you too, hubby. You know I got you. This is us, baby. You and me. Until the death. I love you with all my..." She paused and looked over my shoulder, then pushed me off of her, fumbling back inside of her Gucci bag. "Baby, it's two dudes gettin' out of Guns's car, headin' towards us with their pistols out. Holy shit." She pulled her gun out; cocked it and aimed.

I ducked down, pulling my nine millimeter from under the driver's seat. Cocked it and came up on bidness. Peeked in the rearview mirror and waited until the two dudes got closer to the car. They were hunched over, walking as brisk as the position would allow them to. As soon as they got to the back bumper of the car, I threw open the driver's door, and got right to work, aiming to kill. I knew what their intent was, so I felt it was in my best interest to kick shit off before they had the chance too.

Boom. Boom. Boom.

One head shot. The first dude fell and the other one raised his gun to shoot. He let off one shot in my direction before turning and running away at full speed, with Jade behind him. She stopped halfway and bussed three times. The attacker continued to run, not fazed by her shots. Sirens sounded maybe a few blocks away, just as the snow began to fall from the sky.

"Jade, come on, we gotta get out of here, baby!" I hollered, jumping back into the car, at the same time a police cruiser appeared on the scene. Slamming its brakes, both doors opened. The officers took out their guns and aimed them in our direction from about a half-block away.

I threw our car into reverse and stepped on the gas. *Vroom!* The car sped backwards. In front of us, the police officers jumped back into their cruiser in hot pursuit.

Errrr-uh! I did a backwards U-turn with the car before throwing it into drive, once again stepping on the gas. *Vroom*! In a matter of seconds, we were doing ninety down the residential street, with the police about a block and a half back. I was drive as erratic as possible. All on the sidewalk, then back on to the road. Driving at pedestrians, doing anything that would make them want to call off the chase.

Guns fell on the floor in the back seat. I could smell his stench. The fact that we had a dead body in the back seat, and multiple warrants out for our arrest was enough to make me pull out all of the stops to try and get away. There was no denying it, if we were apprehended, we'd be facing the death penalty. Our lives would be over.

"Baby, you gotta lose them. You gotta lose them. Please!" Jade hollered, pulling her seat belt around her.

I made a hard right and bent a corner, then a left into an alley. Flew down it and hit another right, then another left, flying so fast that I was forced to slam into two garbage cans. They popped into the air and sent trash flying everywhere, before I made another right out of that alley, and into another one right behind the Peter McGuire Projects. Slowed the car, pulled into an abandoned garage and cut the engine.

"What? What are you doing?" Jade hollered.

I took off her seat belt and threw open the driver's door, taking her hand. "Let's go, baby. Come on." We ran out of the alley and across the parking lot to the projects, full speed.

We got to the back entrance of the building, where there were a group of dudes standing in front of it with blue bandannas around their necks. One of them, a big musclebound dude blocked the door, preventing us from running into the building. He held up a hand while his crew settled on the side of him. "Hold fast, cuz. I don't know where the fuck y'all coming from, but y'all ain't coming in this bitch without getting charged a fee."

I stopped in front of him. Look, bruh, let us in and hide us and I got ten thousand with your name on it. You can't beat that." My heart was pounding. The sirens were super loud, and sounded like multiple cars were on the chase. I knew it was just a matter of time before they invaded the expanse of the Peter McGuire Projects.

The big gorilla frowned. "Ten gees. Damn, y'all must be in some serious trouble." He squinted, then his eyes were opened wide. "Wait a minute. Y'all ain't Bentley and Jade, are y'all? Hell n'all, I can't believe it. It is y'all. Cuz, watch out, let them into the building and don't let nobody else come through them doors. Not even twelve." He waved us to follow him.

We jogged through the hallways and took the stairs until we got to the twelfth floor. Once there, we jogged some more, and wound up going to an apartment in the middle of the hallway. A dark-skinned female opened the door in just her bra and panties after the big gorilla-looking dude beat on it three times. She let us in.

He closed the door behind us and pointed to the back room. "Take yo ass back there, shorty, and don't bring yo ass out of that room until I call for you. You understand that?" he ordered Jazzy.

She nodded and rushed into the room. Slammed the door, and that was that. Seconds later, I heard music blaring out of the speakers.

I peeked out of the window and saw three police cars pull into the parking lot of the projects. They jumped out of their whips and rushed toward the building. I fixed the curtain. "Yo, what's yo name, kid?"

"Lethal. What's good wit that ten gees? A deal is a deal," he said, walking to the refrigerator and pulling out a jug of orange juice, twisting the cap and turning the bottle up.

"Yo, you gotta help us get over to the Comfort Inn off of Parkside. That's where the scratch is. We ain't on no bullshit, kid. Twelve came out of nowhere. Mafuckas jump right to it. I gotta bag at the motel. That's where all of our shit is. No bullshit."

He finished downing the juice and replaced it in the refrigerator. Burped and stepped into the living room, sucking on his teeth all loud-like. "Why you ain't tell me all that shit downstairs? Had you told me that down there, I wouldn't have fucked wit y'all. That sound like too much baggage for me. Ten gees ain't even that much scratch to begin with. Not by how twelve sweating y'all ass." He looked out of the front window and down into the parking lot. "Damn, they like twenty deep out there."

The sirens were screaming louder than a white girl in a scary movie. Jade paced back and forth, biting on her forefinger. I worried that all of her stressing could put our child into danger, along with herself.

"Yo, fifteen thousand, bruh. Fifteen thousand just to get us out of these projects and to safety. Now, you can't beat that."

He laughed. "Oh, I could. I'm pretty sure twelve got a nice reward on y'all head, but lucky for y'all I don't fuck wit them like that, and them mafuckas looking for me too. So, I'ma take that fifteen thousand, and help y'all get up of here. Y'all gon have to chill for a few hours, let me work my magic. I'll be right back." He disappeared into the back room and came back five minutes later, with his arm around the dark-skinned female's neck. "Yo, Jazzy gon make sure y'all straight until I get back. Give me a few hours and I'ma move some shit around. Shorty, don't answer this door for nobody." He stepped to me and looked into my eyes. "Fifteen gees, nigga. No less, and no more excuses. Right?" He lowered his eyes almost challengingly.

I nodded. "Right."

"Aiight, I'll be back then." He eyed Jazzy. "Remember what I said."

She smiled and nodded. Closed and locked the door behind him. Added the chain and turned to us. "Are y'all hungry?"

I looked over to Jade. I didn't have an appetite. I was so scared that I was low-key passing gas. But, my baby was pregnant and she needed to eat. "Yo, I'm good, but my wife might be a lil famished."

Jade shook her head and stepped to the window Lethal had been looking out of. Her knees got so weak that they buckled. "Baby, there are police everywhere. We gotta get out of here. We can't wait for him to return. We have to get out of here right now," she said through a shaky voice.

Jazzy, who couldn't have been older than nineteen, stepped into front of me and shook her head. "Nall, Lethal told y'all to chill, so that's what y'all have to do. He's going to buss a few moves that should work in the two of you's favor. Y'all just gotta trust him," she assured.

Jade smacked her lips. "We don't know him. For all we know, he could be somewhere selling us out to the police right now as we speak. He don't owe us no loyalty, and neither do we owe him any. Yo, we about to trust this stud or what, Bentley? Looking down there, it won't be long before the police have this entire building surrounded and are going from door to door."

"You guys have to trust him. If he says he's going to get you out of here, then he will. I've never known him to not be a man of his word. Y'all need to fall back."

18

Jade mugged her and stepped away from me, until she was standing in the girl's face. "Uh, excuse me, but you're supposed to say everything you're saying. That's your man of some sort. We don't know what plan y'all came up with in that room. So, it's in your best interest to carry out his wishes and look out for him. But, you see that handsome, caramel-skinned man over there with those brown eyes? He's in my best interest. That's my husband and I'ma do what's best for him and I, regardless to what you're talking about."

Jazzy took four steps back and held up her hands. "Aiight, cool. Y'all grown as hell. I can't make y'all so nothing you don't want to. All I'm saying is that my nigga is one hunnit. He's thorough, through and throughout. You run a better chance of fuckin' wit him then you do of going at twelve alone. Trust me on that."

I looked out the window again. The parking lot looked like a police station's parking lot. I felt my anxiety shoot through the roof. I imagined us being apprehended. Thrown into the back of a police car, booked on multiple murder charges, and the thought of it was enough to make me sicker than a child with the flu. As fucked up as it was, we were forced to roll the dice. "Yo, shorty, you offered to make us somethin' to eat earlier, right?"

She nodded. "Aw, you hungry now?"

I nodded. "Yeah, why don't you go in there and whip us up a nice lil meal. Give me and my wife some time to talk while we wait on Lethal. Cool?"

Jade frowned and gave me a look that said I must have been out of my mind. "I don't need her to cook for you. All she gotta do is let me go in there, so I can do my own thing. I'll hold my own husband down." She rolled her eyes. Stepped beside me and slid her arm around my lower back.

Jazzy sucked her teeth. "Cool. I don't care. Lethal just said to make sure y'all eat something. I ain't tryna get into all of this drama with you. I'm just following my man's orders. That's it."

"And, that's cool. Why don't you hook us both up some cheeseburgers, fries, you know that whole bit? We'll chat, while we wait on your man to show back up," I said.

She smiled. "Aw, I'm a beast at making that. I gotchu." She turned and walked into the kitchen. Before meeting her destination, she looked over her shoulder at me.

Jade scoffed and attempted to rush into the kitchen behind her, before I grabbed her and pulled her back to me. "Yo, chill, goddess. Leave that bitch alone. We need to get our minds right. Let's think and make this shit happen. We gotta come from under this, boo. We gotta get on to the next chapter of our lives."

Jade continued to mug the girl from over my shoulder. "Yeah, let's do that and get the hell out of here. I don't like how she been peeping you since we got here. On top of that, I don't trust neither one of them. There is a lot of money being offered for us. People will do anything to obtain small amounts of cash, so just imagine what they'll do for a half-million dollars?"

She was right and I knew it. I took another glance out of the project window and saw more squad cars pull into the lot. I became worried. I didn't know how we were going to come from under this sticky situation.

Chapter 3
Jade

I heard the sounds of a key jiggling inside a lock. This made both me and Bentley jump from the couch and back away from the door, with our hands on our pistols. My heart was pounding so hard, I could barely breathe. We'd officially been inside the small apartment for four hours. From as far as I could tell, the police were knocking on the doors to every apartment, along with housing authority officials. I knew from past experience that the housing authority had enough power to give the police permission to enter into any apartment they felt was necessary. This worried me because if they did this, then me and Bentley were screwed.

Bentley pulled me behind him and took his gun out of his waistband. "Yo, Jade, I'm letting you know right now that I ain't about to let us go down like they thinking. I'ma pop this cannon until it's empty, ma. That's my word."

I swallowed my spit, praying we didn't have to resort to anything like that. I'd been shot once before in my life, and it was the worst pain I'd ever felt in my life. I never wanted to experience a pain like that ever again. To imagine the police riddling is with bullets was almost enough to cause me to become hysterical. I held my gun at my side with the hammer cocked back, ready to fire, hating the thought of my life ending within the next few seconds.

Lethal opened the door and came into the apartment in a hurry. He closed the door back and pulled a half-ski mask off of his face. His eyes were wild. "Yo, look, the police on they way up here."

My heart dropped.

"They on they way up here, but I need y'all to chill. I got everything under control," Lethal added, wiping his mouth and looking out of the window.

Bentley snapped, "How the fuck you got everything under control, B? If them people come up in here, ain't nothing you gon be able yo do to stop them from taking us down. Yo, I knew we shouldn't have trusted you. Come on, Jade." He took ahold of my hand and pulled me toward the front door.

Lethal ran and blocked it. "Yo chill, kid. I don't know how y'all do thangs back in New York, but here in Jersey we got a payroll, and every mafuckin' twelve that work around Peter McGuire is on it, one way or the other. Fall back. I got two of the homies about to roll through this bitch. All y'all gotta do is chill in the pantry and let me handle everything else. They ain't gon go that far. Trust me on this. This my homeland. Word up."

Bentley looked down to me with a peculiar look in his face. "What you think, goddess? You wanna take this chance, or do you wanna go for what we know? Ain't no surrendering in my blood, and ain't none in yours either." he said, holding my face in his big hands. Our foreheads were against one another's.

I took a peep out of the window from the corner of my eye. Thought about how many officers were gathered in the parking lot. Tried to imagine what odds we held at getting away from them by going kamikaze and felt sick to my stomach. There was just no way. We'd be filled with so many bullets, it would be ridiculous. It was like I could feel the pain of the gunshot to my thigh reinvent itself, and I knew it was a pain I did not want to endure all over my body. As much as I didn't trust Lethal and Jazzy, we pretty much had to. The alternative was way too dangerous. I

22

took a deep breath and exhaled slowly. "We gotta trust him, baby. We really don't have a choice."

Bentley kissed my forehead. "Are you sure, baby? I'ma give you this call. Anything you wanna do, we gon do."

There was a banging on the door that nearly caused me to jump out of my skin. "Camden Police! We have permission from the housing authority to search these premises."

Bom. Bom. Bom. Bom. Bom.

Lethal rushed to the door. "Say, man, hold the fuck on. Me and my lady getting dressed. Give us two minutes." He turned to Bentley and pointed toward the pantry. "Trust me, bruh. I ain't that caliber of fuck nigga. All I got is my word, and my word is with the god. Nah mean?"

Bentley stared at him for what seemed like a long time. I took his hand and pulled him in the direction of the pantry. "Come on, baby. We ain't got no other choice. We have to remember that God got us. He has the final say." I was just praying he had not released us on the account of the sins that we committed as of late. I mentally prayed he saw the reasoning behind our dealings and forgave us for them.

We settled into the small pantry and crouched down, after closing the door. It smelled like flour and Pine Sol inside, as if someone had recently mopped the floors. The top of my head rested against the bottom shelf. Bentley settled in front of me, always on the ready to catch a bullet for his wife. I loved him so much.

"Baby, if this nigga twist us, and them people rush in here, just surrender and blame everything on me," he whispered. "Yo pops' murder and everything. Tell 'em I did and I'ma stand on that shit. I don't want our child born in a prison, and I ain't about to let you go down. I'm your sacrifice, just like the Bible say, so don't fight me on this. That's an order."

I popped him in the back of the head. "Shut up," I whispered. "Are you out of your mind? What type of wife do you take me for?" I snapped.

"Shssh. You heard what I said. Now just do it. Ain't no reason for the both of us to go down for the same crimes, when I can take the fall for it. You need to focus on having us a healthy baby and having it in prison ain't gon be nothing but a detriment to the both of us and our child." He said this with his lips against my earlobe. His breath tickled the hairs on the inside of my ear canal, before he kissed my neck.

"Look, I don't care what you talking about. We ride together, we die together. Ain't no snitch in me, Bentley, now stop disrespecting me. Far as I'm concerned, everything that you did, I did and vice versa. They can't separate what Jehovah has brought together. That's just that." I whispered and closed my eyes to calm myself. I didn't know what kind of woman Bentley thought he was dealing with, but clearly he had me mistaken. I would never allow for him to take the fall for us. I didn't need a savior. I already had one in Christ. I was just as strong as he was and would never stoop so low as to put everything on him. I was more of a woman than that.

Outside of the pantry, I could hear the sounds of men's voices, then the squeaking of doors opening. Furniture being drug across the floor, and Lethal speaking up, irritated. "Yo, take it easy on my shits, Dunn. I don't know what the fuck y'all looking for, but it ain't in here. Y'all need to bounce, so me and my bitch can go back to sleep. Word up."

More furniture scraped across the floor, maybe a table or the couch. There was squeaking of a door, then there were footsteps in the kitchen. This made me nervous because we were basically in the kitchen, just a few steps to the right of the stove.

"Yo, what the fuck you walking all through my kitchen and shit for, son? Ain't nothing in there for you," Lethal hollered.

"Just peeking around. Calm down. We've been given permission to search the entire expanse of the apartment by the housing authority," said a deep voice. His footsteps came so close to the door of the pantry, I could smell the scent of the man's cologne. It was strong, mixed with a hint of sweat. It made my stomach turn. Suddenly, I felt a wave of what felt like morning sickness come over me. I covered my mouth with my hand.

"Yo, Harris, tell ya mans to get the fuck out of my kitchen, B. Son tracking my floors all up and shit, and we just mopped these joints. Damn."

"Step aside, sir, or I'll be forced to take you down."

"Yo, Harris, call this new jack off."

Silence.

Bentley slid from under the pantry shelf and raised both of his guns, aimed them at the door in preparation. I knew as soon as the pantry door opened, he was going to smoke whatever man was standing in front of it. He appeared to already have his mind made up.

I stood behind him and rubbed his shoulder, then aimed at the door alongside him, ready to follow his lead as the head of our family. His fate would be mine as well. I didn't want to raise a child in this world without the security of Bentley. He and I were one. My love for him was boundless.

"Yo Harris, call off ya dog, man!" Lethal hollered. He sounded irritated.

"Last warning, sir. Move, or I will be forced to take you down," came the deep voice of the police officer.

"Yo, do it then. Word up. You think you finna continue to fuck my crib up, nigga, you got another thing coming. Now, I let y'all search my shit, and whatever you're looking for ain't here. Now get the fuck out or make your next move your best move. Ain't no hoes over here," Lethal retorted, with anger in his voice.

"That's it. It's time somebody taught you some respect."

"Don't pull that Taser out. Don't pull it out. Harris, call ya mans. He pull that Taser out, I'ma be forced to bake this swine. On everythang."

There was scuffling in the kitchen. Shoes squeaked on the linoleum floor.

"Hey! Hey! Knock it off. Jackson! Knock it off!" somebody hollered.

"Come get 'em, B. Come get 'em!" Lethal advised again.

More scuffling and squeaking was heard. "Fuck going on out there?" Bentley asked, backing us all the way toward the rear of the small pantry.

"Yo, get the fuck out of my shit now, B. You supposed to check this rookie. Just 'cause we in the projects don't mean he can treat us like garbage, son. Word up."

"You're supposed to submit to us. We're the law, you son of a bitch!"

"Jackson! Let's go! Do you want another suit slapped against your ass? Now get!"

"But he tried to—"

"Leave now, that's an order!" snapped Harris.

"Fuck!" Jackson cursed and slammed the door so hard that it knocked a bag of sugar off the shelf.

"Sir, thank you for your cooperation. Sorry for the inconvenience. You people have a nice evening."

Harris went on his way. "Yeah, control ya homie, cuz. Shit almost got outta hand. Fuck I'm paying you for?"

"Yeah, I know. That's my bad, but I have to make things look as authentic as possible. Look, we're going to be here for at least another three hours. You might wanna fall back until then. Get your house in order. My apologies once again."

"Yeah whatever, man," Lethal quipped. They continued to talk heading toward the front of the house. Their words became hard for me to make out.

Two minutes later, Lethal opened the door to the pantry. Y'all good in here?"

***

"Look, I'm telling you, you need to fuck wit my cousin down in Miami Gardens. Bruh buss moves back and forth, getting people out of the country all the time. That's his thing. For about fifty gees, he can hook you up wit a nice pad in Havana, Cuba. He's a good nigga, B. In fact, I'm headed down that way at the end of the week, if y'all want, I'll personally introduce you to him. But, I do wanna ask a favor of you, Bentley. You know, just to see what's good."

I sat back on the couch, trying my best to not make eye contact with the dark-skinned chick. I watched the way she peeped Bentley and it was getting on my nerves. She was looking him over with the deepest form of lust in her eyes. They trailed him up and down. Every time he cracked a minor joke, she'd bust up laughing. When he spoke, she was so tuned into him that it had me irate. This bitch was getting under my skin.

Bentley picked up his glass of orange juice and cleared it. As soon as he set the glass on the table, Jazzy jumped up and grabbed it. Took it into the kitchen and refilled it. That further irritated me. She came and set it back in front of him. "Here you go, Bentley." She smiled down at him.

He looked up to her and nodded and looked over to Lethal. "Yo, after what you just did for us, I owe you one. You already got that fifteen coming. What else do you need?"

Lethal pulled on his nose and sniffed hard. "I wanna buss a couple moves down in the three-oh-five that gets me some serious scratch, and your track record precedes you. From what I gather, you're a real cutthroat East Coast nigga. My cousin, Damo, beefing wit a few punks down there that's holding a monopoly on his cash flow. We need to open that up. He's calling in a favor from the god, and I want you to fuck wit me. In exchange, I'll get you and your missus out of the country and on to a new life. Cuz plugged in Havana. Y'all a never have to worry about the states again. That's my word, and the one thing you gon find out about me is that my word is everything and then some." He took three quick pulls from his blunt and inhaled deeply.

"Let me talk this over wit my baby and I'll let you know. She got a say in everything, that's how we get down. Nah mean?" Bentley said, before taking another sip from his glass of orange juice.

Lethal nodded. "That's what's up. Just holler at ya boy." He stood up. "Come on, Jazzy, let them rap for a minute. I need to holler at you back in this room anyway. It's that time of the day, if you know what I mean." He smiled.

She was so busy jocking Bentley that he had to repeat himself before she stood up, and they walked off to the back room. Before they disappeared, she looked over her shoulder to see him one last time. That pissed me off.

T.J. & Jelissa

Chapter 4
Bentley

"Welcome to Cordoba Courts, my nigga. Miami muthafuckin' Gardens in full effect," Lethal said as he pulled his big, money-green Suburban into the parking lot of the row house complex two days later.

Camden had been so hot with twelve all over the place that we'd had to stay cooped up in Lethal's crib for two days straight. The entire time, Jade had been acting real funny. Like something was bothering her, but every time I asked her what the matter was, she held her silence. That was frustrating. I didn't like being locked out from her mentally. We were supposed to be operating as one body.

I looked around at the parking lot that was filled with cars and trucks. It was only five o'clock in the morning. I'd only seen a few people and the sun was just beginning to make its appearance. The wind whistled along, shaking the palm trees. This was the first time in all my life I'd actually seen a palm tree. They looked funny to me.

"Yo, how long you say we gon have to be here, until ya cousin gon be able to buss that Havana move for us?" I asked, with my arm around Jade. She'd been quiet the whole drive and that was unlike her.

"Soon as we handle that lil bidness for him with those cock-blocking ass Haitians, we'll be good to go. That ain't gon take long. All they need is a lil gun play, and it'll be all over. Yo, you gon love the three-oh-five though. Y'all might now wanna go nowhere. Watch." He opened the door to his Suburban, stepped out of it, and knocked on the back window where I was sitting.

I opened the door and jumped out of the whip. Closed it back and stepped over to him. Scanning the area, it looked like your regular everyday row housing projects. The only difference for me was the palm trees scattered about everywhere. "Yo, what's good, bruh?"

He took off walking with me alongside of him. "Yo, we gon have two apartments on their floor. Y'all gon have your own and we gon have ours. The two apartments we're going to be staying in are connected by a door. The door ain't got no lock on it, I'm just letting you know. We shouldn't be down here more than a month though. Is that going to be a problem for you?"

I glanced back at the Suburban and took a deep breath. I didn't know what was going on with Jade. I wanted to go back to the truck and ask her the same question he'd asked me, but I decided against it. What other choice did we have? "Yo, that's cool, just as long as y'all don't have no weirdos stumbling over to our portion. I'm letting you know right now, if I see anything out of the ordinary creeping though our crib with my pregnant wife there, I'm gunning it down ASAP. I ain't gon even think about it. Bussing this gun ain't a math problem, you feel me? There ain't nothin' to figure out. Just aim and squeeze. Been doing it all my life, kid." I wasn't bragging to him, I was just letting him know I was set to get down if I was caught off guard by somebody in our crib. We were a long way from Brooklyn already. I'd never been to Miami before, and I didn't know what to expect. But, I 'd heard from one of the homies back in Brooklyn who was from here, that the cats in Miami got down and dirty just like we did. Had I woken up and a nigga was rummaging through my crib in Brooklyn while my pregnant wife was present, I'da smoked they ass too. It was as simple as that.

Lethal nodded. "Yo, I don't know you from Adam, but I like yo swag, cuz. You'd have every right to pop that iron

32

if that happened, so I'ma do my part to make sure it don't. However, I hope you know the feeling is mutual when it comes to that door. So, y'all be very cautious as well. But anyway, I can't wait to you meet Damo, he's a good nigga. He gon take a shine to you right away. He'll be back from the Dominican Republic in a few days. Until then, here go ya keys. Make yourselves at home. It shouldn't be more than a month," he said, handing me two door keys.

***

Jade dropped the duffle bag of cash we'd gotten from Santana on the floor. We were down to a hundred and eighty thousand dollars, after giving Lethal fifteen for helping us with the police situation back in Camden. She rubbed her temples and closed her eyes.

I walked over to her and rubbed her shoulders from behind. "Baby, what's the matter? You've been so quiet the last few days."

She took a deep breath and exhaled through her nose. "Baby, what are doing here? Why does it feel like we keep going in the same circles over and over again? When will we step outside of this same ol' realm, into a new one?"

I came around and stood in front of her. "Baby, we only gon be down here for a few weeks, then we'll be able to hit it across that water on to a new life. You know how the game go. Everything is in steps. One at a time. This should be our official last one before we leave the United States. I thought we had his understanding already. Why is it bugging you now?"

She shrugged her shoulders. "I don't know. I guess I'm just tired of the same ol', same ol'. I'm ready to start a new life. Tired of depending on other people to make things happen for us. Then, we always have to do somebody a favor. That favor always winds up getting us into more trouble than we were in previously. It's just, I don't know. How much do you trust this Lethal dude anyway?"

"I don't trust no nigga. The only person I trust in this world is you. That's it."

"So, how do you know he isn't setting us up for the bounty on our heads?" she asked, walking over to the gray sofa in the middle of the living room and sitting down.

I followed her over to it and wrapped my arm around her shoulder, pulled her back to my chest. "Baby, if that nigga was gon set us up, he could of did that back in Camden with a parking lot full of police. Why would he do it now? It wouldn't make any sense."

"Our entire journey doesn't make any sense. It's been one problem after the next. I don't trust him or that broad, but I'ma let you run the show, until I see a need for me to step in and shut it down. I take it since we gon be staying here for a few weeks that we gon get a few things to make this living arrangement inhabitable? Right?"

I laughed. "For sure. Whatever you want, boo. You already know how it is when it comes to you. How are you feeling in regards to Guns's murder? Any side effects yet?"

She shrugged her shoulders. "Not really. I'm still reeling over Santana's more than anything and I think that's only because I was a bit more familiar with him. Whereas with Guns, I barely knew him and I never trusted him from day one. So, it is what it is. But, thank you for asking." She turned all the way around and straddled my lap. "You know what I do need, though? Something that's going to help me ease my mind," she asked, kissing my lips.

I sucked on her bottom one, before I tongued her down and squeezed her breasts inside her coat. Unzipped it and pulled it open. "What's that, boo?"

She licked my lips and pushed me backward, pressed down on my shoulders until I was between her legs. Once there, she opened them wide and unbuttoned her jeans, before sliding them down her thick thighs. "I need you to taste me. Need you to eat this attitude up out of me, before I shop a lil bit."

I situated myself on my knees, pulled her jeans down to her ankles and off one of them, licked along her inner thigh, all the way to her panties. Once there, I trailed my tongue up and down the crotch band, tasting her through the satin. Yanked it to the side and exposed her meaty sex lips that blocked the entrance to her garden. "Oh, you need a lil head, Jade. Then you wanna go shopping, right?" I laughed. "I gotchu. You know I gotchu." I took my thumbs and held her lips apart. Then my tongue was in her crease, licking it up and down, sucking the pearl into my mouth, tracing circles around over and over, slurping at her juices loudly.

She grabbed the back of my head and forced me further into her center, rising from the couch riding my face swiftly. "Un. Un. Aww, baby. Yes. Eat me. Eat your baby." She threw her legs on my shoulders and leaned all the way back. Moaning and squeezing her own breasts. Her juices were leaking out of her rapidly.

"Cum in my mouth, Jade. Cum on my tongue." More slurping and licking and her ass rose from the cushions of the sofa again and again. My face was a mess and I loved it, loved to feel her juices running down and dripping off of my chin. The rivers of her essence even dared to travel the expanse of my neck on down to my collarbone. It drove me nuts. I trapped her little jewel and sucked harder, needing to feel her cum. I yearned for the sweet and savory taste of her.

She threw her head back and moaned deep within her throat, before cumming all over me, bucking into my mouth. Her legs released themselves from around my shoulders, and she tried to push me away. "Okay. Okay, baby. That's enough. That's enough, it's sensitive."

I continued to keep her thighs trapped, sucking all over them. She was so strapped. I loved everything about her perfect body, loved to worship her temple.

***

Jade had a pep in her step as we walked through Dolphin Plaza Mall, right off of Northwest Twenty-Seventh. She was beaming. That made me feel good, because I hated to see my rib all down and shit. I strived to keep her happy, and all of the bags in her hand was most definitely helping her with that. She stopped in front of Lady Footlocker and looked into the store. "Baby, it already feel like spring down here. I need to get me a few pairs of tennis shoes. Come on. I like those pink and black retro Jordans they got in the display window. They just came out in January of twenty-nineteen. They fresh. What you think?"

I stepped into the store as she held the shoes in her hands, looking them over. I knew from the history Jade had given me about her family that she'd never had the opportunity to even rock a pair of Jordans. If we'd bought the pair she was holding, these would have been her first pair. I felt honored to snatch them up for her.

"Yo, snatch them up and the one in purple and black over there. Matter fact, get four pair. We gotta go back and get a couple outfits to rock wit 'em. I'ma hit up Footlocker and get me the same ones in men. We in the three-oh-five now. This is one of the fashion capitals of the world. We gotta look the part."

She smiled. "I agree. All of that ripping and running and we never get a chance to do anything. Lord knows, we could have gotten caught back there in Camden and would have had nothing to show for it. No travel, no outings, no fun. I say if we gon live this fast life, well at least until the baby comes, then we should splurge just a lil bit. We been broke and poor this whole time." She walked up to one of the female sales clerks. She was a slim, white girl, with long blonde hair and a heavily made-up face. "Yes, can I have these in a size seven in women's, and in every color that you have? Thank you."

The white girl nodded. "Sure thing. I'll be right back." She walked off.

Jade stepped into my arms and hugged my body. "I love you so much, baby. You got me feeling so good. You know I gotta hit up LC's Nails and Spa that's right down the way from Footlocker. I need to feel like a girl for a few hours. You cool with that, right, baby?"

I kissed her lips again, loved kissing them juicy blessings. "It's yo world, ma. Whatever it's gon take for you to be cool and stress-free, I'm all for it. After you get right, I want some of that body in the worst way. Now how that sound?"

She laughed and stepped into my face. "Like a plan, baby. Like a heck of a plan.'' Her arms slid around my neck and our lips were locked into an embrace, as the salesgirl walked up with five shoe boxes in her hands. Jade broke our kiss and stood back

"Okay, here you are, miss. Here are all the Jordans of this kind we have in your size."

Jade nodded. "That's what's up. We'll be up there to pay for them in a second. Baby, before we lay our heads tonight, we should have our bed, right? Didn't the man say they'll have it over to us before the day is out? I sure don't feel like sleeping on nobody's floor, or even that old worn couch. I feel like we've done that enough. We need to enjoy life at least a tad bit more. Don't you think?"

I nodded and watched the salesgirl try her best to juggle the shoes all the way to the front of the store. She stumbled more than once, before she gingerly made it to the front. Set them on the counter and looked back to see what we were doing. I peered into Jade's pretty brown eyes. "Baby, I agree with you and I know you're tired of struggling, so from here on out we're going to live life to the fullest. I ain't about to let you sleep on no more floors, used beds or couches, no more. Not as long as you have our baby inside of you. Ain't none of that good for it anyway. Second to that, I love you, and you're supposed to have the best of the best anyway. So, just let me do my thing. Okay?"

She nodded and pulled me down to her face, so she could kiss my lips again. Sucked on them, then pecked them three times in a row. There was a loud smacking noise that emitted from us. "Aiight then, I'ma let you do your thing, baby. Spoil me. After all, I deserve it."

Chapter 5
Jade

Three weeks after we'd been in Miami, and without any word as to when Lethal's cousin would be showing up, Bentley came into the apartment with a single rose in his hand, and a look of frustration. He handed me the rose and sat on the couch across from me, with his head down.

I smelled the rose and smiled, before sliding over to his side of the living room until I was sitting next to him, starting to rub his back. "Thank you for the rose, baby. Now tell me, what's the matter with you?"

He shook his head. "Yo, this fool Damo got jammed up on some other stuff down in the Dominican Republic. Ain't no telling when that nigga gon break that seal from down there. In the meantime, Lethal got a bunch of moves lined up to get our cash all the way up. I'm just feeling some type of way about them. I wasn't expecting to be down here this long. I thought after three weeks, we would have at least been a few days out from jumping on a boat. Nah mean?"

I agreed with him. "Yeah, baby, I know. So did I. But so far, it's been pretty relaxed down here. We haven't had any trouble so far. The people down this way have been cool. None of them appear to know who we are. We've fully furnished this place and I gotta tell you, for the first time since we've been on the run I actually feel comfortable some place." I rubbed his back and laid my head on his shoulder. "Everything happens when it's supposed to. We both know that. We'll be okay."

He jerked his head back and looked me over closely. "Wait a minute. Baby, why are you so calm about everything? Yo, I ain't never seen you this chill before. You're usually the one that is freaking out, and I'm calm. You must really like it down here, huh?"

I held out my freshly manicured fingers and glanced down to my French-pedicured toes that matched my digits. This had been the first time in a long since I'd actually felt like a girl or pampered in the slightest. The first three weeks of Miami had felt like a slice of heaven to me. The city was a major change from that of Brooklyn. "Honestly, baby, I like it here. I wished we didn't have to go anywhere at all. Besides, we don't know what another country is like and if we'll be able to survive in one of them. My Spanish is not that great, is yours?"

He stood up and looked down on me, ran his hand over his thick waves. "Yo, goddess, what are you saying? Are you saying you wanna start our family right here in Florida, instead of going across that water?" he asked, looking confused.

I stood up and slid my hands around his waist. "Lethal is going to get us better identifications, and paperwork. He said he has a guy that will make us some that will blow the ones we have now out of the water. So, why wouldn't we take them and start out lives anew right here? I mean, if things get to looking crazy, we could always sail away then."

He broke our embrace and stepped away from me. "Because we ain't got no more strikes, Jade. The first time them people find out where we are, they are going to come with everything they have. Our bounties are up to seven hundred and fifty thousand dollars apiece. They're making us out to be some cold blooded killers. Like we been smoking niggas with no regard for humanity. Got both of our fingerprints off of the car they found Guns' body in. Then, his lil young bitch making it seem like she heard you and I talking about killing him just because. Baby, we're in a bind and the longer we stay in the United States, the slimmer our chances are at finding forever, with each other and our child. We have to get out of here as soon as we can. Do you understand that?"

As much as I hated to admit it, he was right. It was only a matter of time before they tracked us down to Miami. Even though neither of us had any ties that led there, it was still a part of the United States of America. I sighed and sat back on the couch and hung my head. "Yeah, I know. You're right. I saw the *World News* this morning and they had a short snippet about us on there. Broadcast our pictures from various times and everything. So, I guess we're back to planning how we're going to get across that water, huh?"

He slid beside me and placed his arm around my shoulder. "Yeah, baby. But, from what Lethal saying, it might take his cousin Damo a few more weeks before he's able to come from under that jam that he's in, so we're definitely going to be here longer than we planned on being. And while we're here, we'll enjoy ourselves. I'll boss a few moves with him, so we can gross a lil more paper, and by the time we set sail we should be all the way up. Aiight, ma?" He kissed my cheek, then placed his hand on my stomach. Rubbing it in a circular motion.

"Baby, can we go out. You know, like to one of those clubs on South Beach that we used to hear so much about back home? Or, maybe even Disney World? Wait, it ain't safe for me to be getting on rides while I'm pregnant. So, that's out of the question, and clubbing seems a bit ambitious as well. Dang, we can at least go to the beach. I wanna feel the effects of Florida while we're here. I didn't wanna be all cooped up in the house like I've been in every other city. That makes me so depressed. I'm not even kidding." I wasn't going for it either. I was tired of feeling like a prisoner, waiting for our demise, and being ducked off in some apartment during the waiting process, fearing the unknown. Looking over my shoulder every second of every day was driving me crazy.

"Baby, that's cool. Whatever you wanna do, we can do. I just need to get an understanding with Lethal to see what kind of moves he got on the table, but for now you gone 'head and get dressed, so we can head down to the beach. It's seventy-five degrees outside and supposed to be in the low eighties."

I hopped up, all giddy-like. Anytime it was time to get out of the house, I was all for it.

***

Two hours later, there was a big sun hat on my head. A picnic basket in my hand, and with every step that I took the warm white sand leaked between my toes. The waves of the ocean were big. They sailed to the shore before wetting it and disappearing. The sun shined bright in the blue sky. A flock of seagulls flew through the air, squawking loudly. The beach appeared to be packed with multiple women laying face-down on their beach towels topless, a G-string splitting the cheeks of their backsides. There were a few men throwing a football back and forth, shirtless. The sun reflected off of their heavily baby-oiled and chiseled bodies. There were a bunch of people jogging along the beach. Some held dog leashes in their hands. Their dogs jogged beside them, barking every few yards. There was a light breeze that smelled salty.

Bentley wore a pair of Ray-Ban sunglasses. I didn't know where his eyes were looking but there was so much barely covered female flesh on the beach, I could only imagine how many of the chicks he visually drank in. He pointed up ahead. "Yo, there go that nigga Lethal and Jazzy right there. Damn, this fool done hooked up him a whole ass cabana." He shook his head and increased his long strides, almost leaving me behind. Looked back to me and slowed again. "You want me to carry our picnic basket, ma?"

I was so irritated looking ahead. Jazzy stood in front of the cabana, in just a two-piece Fendi bathing suit. She rubbed oil on her chocolate body. The sun reflected off of her silky skin. Her butt was poked out like a full stomach, her waist small and breasts fully plump and just as chocolate as the rest of her. Her natural curly hair fell to her shoulders.

"Nall, baby, I got it. Honey, why we have to have our first beach experience with them? I just wanted it to be me and you," I said, still eyeing the chocolate girl. I didn't know why, but she had me feeling all kinds of insecure. The closer we got to them, the more I started to see just how stacked she was, and every other female on the beach it seemed, for that matter. I truly wondered if Bentley peeped all of that.

We were about twenty feet away from them now, stepping last a bunch of people that were laid out in the sand listening to their music, or simply dozing on their towels. The wind blew my hair off of my shoulders. Small particles of sand invaded the air, causing me to squint my eyes.

"Ma, you should have said something. I just thought it would be cool if we all chilled. That way we can get to know them a lil better and vice versa. We basically sharing an apartment with them and know very little about them. If you want us to do our own thing, then we can. I'll just spin they ass real quick. You want me to?"

I watched Jazzy turn around and shake out a beach towel. Her ass jiggled, along with her hefty thighs, then she bent over

43

and spread the towel on the sand. The crotch band of her thong basically disappeared. I looked up to Bentley and saw that he was looking down on her. His eyes could not miss what I'd seen and it had been a lot. "Baby, is you looking at that bitch right now?" I asked, stopping in mid stride.

"What? Who, ma?"

"Don't play dumb. You know who I'm talking about." I pulled down my Chanel shades and glared up at him.

He looked off. "Damn, goddess, it ain't nothing like that. I mean, the lil bitch came into my line of vision, but I ain't jocking her like that, if that's what you mean. I got a whole-ass bad wife right here. Flawless. And you carrying my seed. What type of nigga would I be?" He sighed. "Yo, if you ain't feeling us jamming wit them, then we can go to the other side of the beach. My whole reason for stepping out today is so I can make you happy, so if you ain't, then we can do something else."

Lethal threw his arms up. He was without a shirt as well. He was built like a heavyweight boxer. Tatted up like crazy. Muscles bulging out of everywhere, just like Bentley. "'Bout time y'all showed up?"

"So we good baby, or what do you wanna do?" Bentley asked.

Jazzy laid on her stomach and placed the side of her face on her arms. The sun seemed to shine bright off of her backside. She'd already loosened the strings of her two-piece top. Her round globes displayed themselves under each arm.

"We can chill for a lil while, but if I get to feeling some type of way, we're out of here. Understand?" I pulled his glasses off of his face so he could look directly into my eyes.

He nodded. "Yeah, I understand. It's all good, boo. Now come on, let's have us a good time."

**

We'd been chilling on the beach for about two hours, when Lethal and Bentley got up and walked away from the cabana, so they could talk about business. I was in the middle of eating one of the turkey and cheese sandwiches that I'd packed for me and Bentley when Jazzy sat up from her beach towel and looked back at me, smiled and got up. She came under the big umbrella of the cabana and grabbed a tropical punch juice out of the cooler. "You don't like me, do you?" she asked, twisting the top off of the juice and taking a swallow.

"I don't know you. You ain't did nothing to me for me to feel one way or the other about you. Life is too short."

She laughed. "Yeah, I'm used to females not liking me. I don't do nothing to them, they just instinctively don't like me. But, it's good." She looked out toward Bentley and Lethal. Licked her lips and shook her head.

I followed her gaze to see Bentley pull his wife beater over his head. The rays of the sun reflected off of his muscular, tattooed body. Even from where I sat, I could see all eight of his ab muscles.

Jazzy rubbed her neck, and then her stomach. Shook her head again and exhaled. "Damn."

"Bitch, maybe other females don't like you because of how you be jocking their men. You ever think about that?" I snapped, ready to jump out of my lounge chair and whoop her ass over the way she was lusting after Bentley.

She shook her head to snap out of her zone. "Aw, damn, girl. I ain't mean to make it so obvious, but yo nigga fine. I know I ain't the first female to tell you that. I mean, look at his stomach, damn."

Bentley ran his hand over his abs unconsciously as he stood and talked with Lethal. Scanning the beach, I could see a few females eyeing him from a distance and pointing, which made me feel even more insecure. It was like they could tell he wasn't from the south or something.

I jumped out of the chair and stepped up into her face. "Yeah, well, you can look but if you know what's in your best interest, you'd stay away from my husband. That's your first and final warning."

She smacked her lips and took five steps back. "Girl, please. Ain't nobody scared of you and yes, I know you're wanted and supposed to be some big-time killer. So what? That don't spook me because I get down too. Trust me when I tell you that. Lethal would never keep me at his right hand if I wasn't 'bout that life." She peered out to the pair. "Yo nigga make my pussy stay wet. Ain't no man ever been able to do that just off the sight of him. But, he do." She slowly trailed her eyes over to me. "And you do too. If you get out of your own way, I could blow both of yall's minds."

"Bitch, what?" My fists were balled. I was ready to smash something. Had I not seen Bentley and Lethal about twenty steps away, I would have snapped on her ass. But, I held my tongue. I didn't know what Lethal and Bentley had discussed, and I didn't want to screw it up. Lethal was our only hope at fresh identities and sailing across the water. I would file away the things that Jazzy had said to me and get at her later.

Before they came all the way back to the cabana, Jazzy bang over and knelt on her towel. "Before y'all leave us,

Jade, I'ma get fucked by him, and taste that pussy of yours. Mark those words."

Chapter 6
Bentley

"Aiight, bruh, now listen to me closely. This move we about to buss gon bring us fifty gees apiece, cash. It's gon be a few bricks of that boy in it too. Since cuz fighting his way out of a sticky situation, me and you might as well get our bands all the way up. If you fuck wit me the long way, I can have us a lick lined up that a gross at least fifty apiece, every single week. One thing about Miami is that it's sweet. Everybody out here having that gwop. The living is fast, and so is the come-ups. We just have to be smart or else a mafucka a knock our heads off quick. Just like back home in Jersey and New York," Lethal said, chopping through a zip of China, then making two thin lines. He leaned his face to the side and tooted them both hard, one line up each nostril, before pulling his head back and pulling his nose. "Fuck, that's that shit." He pushed the platter over to me and nodded. "Try that."

I looked down at it and shook my head. "I'm good, B. I know what that shit do and I ain't in no position to be catching no habits. My wife pregnant and I got a shorty on the way. Everything has to be about advancing."

Lethal took the platter back and grunted. "You in Miami now. Everybody got a habit down here. You'll pick one up sooner or later. Trust me on that."

"Nigga, my habit is money, and advancing. Ain't shit finna change that. Now, what's good with this lick, what does it entail?"

"Knocking off a couple heads. You already know. Two of the power players that's in my cousin's way gotta go. He done already sent word. I got all of the information I need. The layout is fifty gees, and we get to keep any of the packs and cash we find up in there." He sucked his teeth. "We gon pull an old-fashioned kick door. Split some tomatoes and call it a night. Check these out." He got up and left the room. When he came back, he was carrying a long blue trunk with gold trimming. Set it in front of his couch and popped it open. Pulled out an old school AK-47 and handed it to me. Back in Brooklyn, we called them Bin Laden's.

I took the Kay and stood up with it. Pressed the handle against my shoulder and aimed at his wall, pulling the trigger. "Yo, this bitch lit, son. Where the clip at?"

"Shid, I got a hunnit-round one, a fifty-round one, and that one I just gave you a spit a rapid thirty. Every time you touch that trigger, it spit three bullets at a time. The barrel is already equipped with a noise reduction system so the shots will be muffled, and it's about eighty percent accurate from a distance as far as a half a block. I ain't looking forward to us capping nothing from that far away. I expect us to be up close and personal, but it's nice to know that if we had to we could, nah mean? Oh, and here." He grabbed a knapsack from behind him and tossed it over to my side of the couch. "From here on out, you are Pierre Thomas, and she is Jade Thomas. Y'all are from Great Britain, and you just got your green card a month ago. This should keep y'all safe for at least six months," he said, scratching his inner right forearm. "I told you, kid, my word is bond."

I grabbed the cards out of the sack and looked them over. "Damn, that was fast. But, what do we do after the six months?"

He closed his eyes and leaned back on the couch. "You shouldn't be in Miami nowhere close to that. Hopefully, cuz come from out that jam in the Dominican Republic and we can have y'all set sail within the next eight weeks. At least, that's what I'm hoping. In the meantime, we gotta set this city on fire. Squeeze as much cash out of it as possible before cuz get back. You feel me? Damn, I'm tired." He yawned and smacked his lips together, got up and headed toward the back room. "I need about an hour. Foil that work up so we can hit some of these China heads out here. We gon split that merch down the middle as well. I gotta make a run to Jersey tonight, and we'll try and hit this lick I was just telling you about at the end of the week." He yawned again. "Damn, I'm tired. I'ma send shorty out here to help you. She should be woke by now." He disappeared into the back room.

Jazzy came out of the room in a pair of pink Victoria's Secret boy shorts so small, they were all up in her gap. She wore a tank top that stopped just below her breasts. Both brown nipples were visible through the material. In her hand was a whole brick of China. "Hey, Bentley, you need some help bussing all this stuff down?" She sat on the couch across from me and set the brick on the table, peeling open the silver aluminum foil package.

I was a bit irritated. "I didn't even know I was finna bag this shit up. Bruh just sprung this on me, so hell yeah, you can help. You gon do most of the work," I joked, though I was more serious than she realized.

She licked her juicy lips. They were heavily coated with some kind of lip gloss. "It's all good, daddy. I'm used to doing all of the work. Taking the brunt of the load is my forte." She smiled and crossed her thick thighs. The shorts seemed to disappear.

My eyes bugged out of my head. Jade's face flashed into my mind, an angry one. I already knew what she'd do if she even thought I was lusting after this lil chocolate thing before me. "Yeah, well let's get to work. Huh." I handed her a razor blade and a pair of latex gloves. When she leaned over to get them, I caught an unwanted glance down her shirt all the way to her areolas, before closing my eyes tight.

She laughed. "You're funny."

I opened my eyes and looked over at her. "How so?"

She shook her head. "Don't worry about it. Didn't you use to go to Malcolm Shabazz High back in twenty-four-teen, and all the way up until twenty-seventeen? Had a mans named Santana?"

"Yeah, shorty, how you know all of that?" I pulled one of the digital scales closer to me and started to weigh the product on it.

She giggled and shook her head. "Yo, you use to fuck wit my girl, Keri. She was always jacking about you. Talking about how fly you were. How you was out there getting money even when we were freshmen. And of course, how you put it down in the bedroom. You was like the talk of our lil crew. Good ol' Bentley."

I sat dumbfounded trying to remember her face, but for the life of me could not place it, and I made sure I paid attention to every bad bitch that walked the halls of Malcolm Shabazz. Keri was by far the coldest, but Jade was right there with her. Keri was mixed with black and Puerto

50

Rican, whereas Jade was all sista as far as I knew. After them, the school was up for grabs. There had been a lot of bad dark skinned sistas too, but I was sure I had never seen Jazzy before. She was cold. I would have remembered her, and probably would have smashed more than once. "Yo, you went to Malcolm Shabazz?"

She shook her head. "Nall, I'm from Flatbush. I went to Phyllis Wheatley. But, we all kicked it together after school, mostly at Coney Island. Me and Keri still real tight to this day. She was my first female, well, you know." She blushed and started foiling and bagging the work.

"Yo first what? You might as well say that shit now that you brought it up." I wanted to hear this, because a few years back when Santana was having threesomes on a regular basis, I got jealous and asked Keri if she'd have a few of them with me, to which she declined. She said she ain't get down with broads like that, and she felt a sexual relationship was supposed to be strictly between two people that loved each other. I got so irritated I started having them without her.

Jazzy shrugged her shoulders. "Keri used to stay a lot of nights at my house when we were in high school, because her people were always drink and fighting one another. Ninth, tenth, and even our eleventh grade years were some of our most curious times, so we played around and got real familiar with each other." She uncrossed her thighs, cocked them wide open, and rubbed her inner left thigh, right by the crotch band that was all up in her cat. So much so that I could see her brown sex lips peeking out of each side of the material. She dared to run a finger over one of them, before crossing her legs again.

Damn. I felt my piece hardening. I felt guilty. Her perfume made its way to my nostrils. Her nipples were rock hard and spiked up against her tank top.

51

"We used to get so hot because of all the stories she'd tell me about y'all, and the stuff y'all did to each other. We'd have our legs hooked up, bumping kitties while she moaned and talked, until we couldn't take it no more. I'd been getting off to you long before we ever met, Bentley. Is that weird?" Her thighs were spread again. She took the material and pulled it all the way into her gap. Now both of her lips were fully exposed. She even dared to take her right foot and set it on the couch, bussing her cat wide open.

I couldn't take my eyes away from her middle. She rubbed the center until a damp spot appeared there. My dick jumped in my pants. I was in a trance-like state.

"Keri said you like thick hoes, Bentley. Them project goddesses. Well, look at all of this." She turned around, placed both knees on the sofa and bent over. Her cheeks hung out of the shorts. She slid her hand under her stomach and rubbed along her lips. "I wish you could fuck me like you did her. I been wanting a piece of you since I was fourteen, and you so damn fine. Look at all this." She spread her knees further and pulled the shorts upward, exposing more of herself.

With lightning speed, I dipped my hand into my boxers and grabbed my piece and adjusted it, before standing up. "Yo shorty, my word, you bad as hell and I can't take that from you but Jade my baby girl. I can't flex on her like that. Our bond is deeper than sex. Whatever fantasies Keri done put in your brain, you gotta let that shit go. I belong to Jade, so if you wanna fuck wit me in that capacity, you gotta holler at her."

She sat back down and opened her legs, slid her hand into her shorts. "Made just as fine as you are, I'd love to give you that threesome that Keri was afraid to. All you gotta do is get your baby mama on board, and it's a go."

"Shorty, Lethal gone beat yo ass talking like that and if he don't, then Jade will. And for the record, she ain't just my baby mother, she's my wife." I grabbed my jacket and slid it on, wrapped up about a half a brick to take care of it when I got back to my crib. I had to get away from Jazzy. She was a temptress, and I was still only eighteen. Learning how to control my southern head had always been difficult, until I fell in love with Jade.

"Lethal don't dictate what I do. I'm my own person. And, as far as your wife goes." She did air quotes with her fingers. "She already know I'm feeling the both of y'all. Why it can't be what happens in Miami stays in Miami? I already got your dick hard. What's really good?" she asked, crossing her thighs again. Now her nipples were really poking through the shirt. She kept on moving around on the couch as if she was uncomfortable.

"Yo, I'm out, shorty. Tell Lethal I took a half of brick. I'ma handle this bidness when I get to the crib. I'ma send him a text too." I got out of there as fast as I could, with her laughing behind me.

T.J. & Jelissa

Chapter 7
Jade

"Ma! Ma! Where you at, baby?" Bentley called as I stepped out of the shower and wrapped a pink terrycloth bath towel around my shoulders. I'd just taken a nice long steam shower and took the twisted dreads out of my head. My natural hair flowed just below my shoulders nice and thick. I had booked an appointment to have it done first thing in the morning.

"I'm in here, baby. In the bathroom!" I hollered, opening the door.

Bentley came down the hall, stopped in front of me, and looked me up and down. "Yo, you took your dreads out?"

"Yeah, I told you I wanted to do this a long time ago. What do you think?"

He eyed me from head to toe and snatched the towel from my body, then picked me up. My legs automatically wrapped themselves around his body. He held me against the wall and sucked all over my neck, sending chills down my spine. My breathing became ragged. "You're bad, baby. You so fucking bad." He carried me to our room and laid me on to the big king sized bed. Kneeling, and kissing each one of my little toes, before sucking them into his mouth one at a time. Pausing in between sucks to talk to me. "I got the baddest woman on the planet." Sucking and sucking. "You make me so happy, Jade." More sucking, making his way up my body where he spread my thighs and kissed all over my kitty, licking in between the lips, sucking on each one individually, and them both of them together. I could feel my cream ooze into his mouth.

"My clit, baby. Open me up and get my jewel." I watched him in action.

He spread my kitty lips until my pink revealed itself. Took his tongue and licked up and down each wall as far as he could reach. Then he made quick circles around my pearl tongue over and over, before sucking it into his mouth, treating it like a nipple.

I humped into his face, grabbed the back of it, riding it like a jockey. "Uh, baby. Baby. Yeah. Eat me. Eat your wife. Eat me, honey. Heaven yes!" I gasped, moaning with all of my might as he worked magic on my jewel. In a matter of minutes, I was flopping around riding his face like a mermaid getting head. Pushed all of the pillows on to the floor, it was that damn good. "I'm cumming! I'm cumming! I'm cumming, Bentley. Uh shit, honey!" My legs opened wide as I humped up from the bed and rode his face into oblivion.

Minutes later and with my juices leaking out of me, I laid him on his back and took his big dick in my hand, stroking it up and down. It was so thick and heavy. I still couldn't believe I'd ever been able to take all of it. I loved my husband so much. I pulled down on the stalk and ran my tongue in circles all around the crabapple-sized head, then sucked him into my mouth. Sucking and stroking him with my left hand, I popped it out and trailed my tongue along the underside of it. Sucked his right ball into my mouth and then the left one, licked up to his head, and sucked that back into my lips. Then I was spearing my face into his lap at full speed, while he groaned and made weird noises with his eyes closed tightly.

"Uh, Jade. Un, ma. Fuck, baby. Do that shit. Do that shit, my rib." He rose from the bed and worked his dick in and out of my mouth. It was so long at this point that every time I tried to swallow it whole, I wound up gagging.

He reached over my back and slapped my naked ass. Cuffed it and fondled the cheeks. Then, he was playing the lips of my cave, before his finger slipped into my oven like a loaf of bread. "Damn, you so thick."

"Uh! Bentley. Please cum in my mouth, baby. Let me swallow you. Please." I got to sucking him so fast, he started to whimper. I knew I had that ass then.

"Baby. Baby. Aw, fuck. I'm cumming. I'm cumming," he said, shaking like he was having a seizure.

His cum flew into my mouth in squirts. I pumped his dick to get more of it. Sucking the head and running my fist up and down his massive tool, squeezing it in my fist, milking him until he was dry. Then I started to suck him back to full mass. "I need some of this dick, baby. Need you to put it down. Can you handle that?" I teased.

He pulled out of my mouth and bent me over the bed. Got behind me and smacked me on the ass cheek hard. "I want this shit from the back. You finna take me like that. Gimme this pussy." He kicked my legs apart and guided his piece into me. I could feel my sex lips opening to accept the full length of him. When his balls landed against my clit, it felt as if he was inside of my stomach. He pulled back and slammed forward again, and then he was fucking me like a porn star. Holding my hips while my breasts slapped against my stomach and rubbed against the blanket of the bed.

"This my pussy, Jade. Mine. I'm finna kill this shit."

Clap. Clap. Clap.

"Uh! Uh! Uh! Uh! Uh!" I pushed back into his lap over and over, feeling him sink deeper and deeper into my womb. I closed my eyelids tightly together and started to moan so loud, I was sure the neighbors next door could hear me as clear as day, and I didn't even care.

He pulled out and tossed me back on the bed, got between my legs, and reinserted himself into my womb, pounding at full speed while my manicured nails were all over his back.

He sucked my neck and licked the sweat from it. The head-board continued to crash into the wall as if it were trying to go through it. Bentley was a maniac in my pussy. In a zone, one I'd never seen him in before.

He flipped me on my side, played with my jewel and stroked me hard and rapidly. Approximately ten minutes passed before I had all that I could take. I screamed I was cumming again, began to shake worse than an earthquake in California. This must have brought on his climax, because seconds later, I could feel his hot seed spilling into me. He grunted and dug his fingers into my hips jerking again and again.

***

The next morning, I got up bright and early so I could make my nine o'clock hair appointment I'd booked with Lisa of Lisa's Beauty Salon. Got my hair washed and conditioned, before she sat me down to whip it in the style I'd pointed out to her from the catalog on her website. It felt so good to once again be getting pampered. I was slowly beginning to understand what it felt like to be a lady, and why I'd always hear my mother complain that she wished she could go out and get her hair and nails done. I breathed a sigh of comfort and closed my eyes as Lisa combed out my hair, before applying the relaxer to it.

"Girl, you got a good grade of hair. It's nice and healthy. You sure you're all black?" the heavyset Asian and black woman asked, parting my hair.

"As far as I know. My mother and father both looked all black to me. My grandmother on my father's side is a bit yellow, and got a million freckles all over her face, but other than that I don't know."

"Well chile, whoever gave you this good grade of hair blessed you. You oughta be thankful. You sure you wanna mess it up with all of these chemicals and thangs?" She held a nice portion of it and tilted my head, so she could look into my eyes.

"I just want to feel like a queen. I don't care about the chemicals, or none of that. I took my dreads out, it's time to turn over a new leaf. Beautify me." I smiled and sat still.

Another one of the beauticians laughed. "Have you ever thought about modeling or being in one of those videos they always shooting on South Beach? You are gorgeous, honey. I betchu can make a whole lot of money, and fast too." She was tall, and light-skinned, and didn't look so bad herself.

"Nall, I never have. Besides, it's so many pretty girls down here, I would feel insecure trying to compete. I ain't seen an ugly person here in Miami yet."

"Girl, keep looking, you bound to see a whole bunch of 'em," Lisa cracked, laughing so loud in my ear that I wanted to elbow her ass.

"I know that's the truth," the tall, yellow beautician said. "Girl, where are you from any way? You sound different."

My head got to spinning so fast to tell a lie that I wound up telling the truth. "I'm from New York. The Big Apple."

"New York. Well, well, well, welcome to the south, baby, you gone love it down here. Everybody is very welcoming. You shouldn't have no problem fitting right in. You plan on being down here for a while? Or are y'all already spring breaking up there?" Lisa asked, going to work on my hair now.

"I'm looking to stay. I like it so far, and so does my husband."

"Husband? A pretty lil young thang like you? Already? Girl, you can't be older than twenty. You must got you one of them rich white boys, or a ball player, huh?" the tall yellow sista asked, brushing her sandy red hair out of her face.

"Nope, my man works in construction, laying bricks," I lied. "He got family down here and wanted to be close to his mother. She's sick."

"But married though? Girl, you got your whole life ahead of you. You ain't supposed to be letting some man tie you down," Lisa said, smearing the thick, funky chemical into my scalp. "How old are you?"

I felt like Lisa was a bit nosey for her own good, but once again before I could form a lie in my mind, I wound up telling her the truth. "I'm eighteen. I'll be nineteen next month on the tenth."

"Oh, girl, and you pregnant. I just noticed that. Yeah, well maybe you better gon 'head and walk down that aisle. Besides, them construction workers make real good money. Twenty-five dollars an hours and that's just to start. A girl can build herself a real nice life with a man making money like that."

"I don't need his money though. I'm my own woman. I can provide for myself. Besides, me and my husband are a team. We make it happen together. Nah mean, goddess?"

Lisa smiled, and looked me over. "That's real cute. Every woman wanna act like they ain't chasing a nigga with some money. I get it. It's all about being independent. Women are equal. Blah, blah, blah. I don't care how equal I am to a man, I ain't messing wit his ass if he broke. That's just that. He gotta be able to meet me more than halfway, and I damn sho ain't marrying his ass if he broke. Lawd have mercy, I ain't," she scoffed. "Now, you one of them New York City gals, y'all some of the biggest gold diggers around. I know that man gotta have something going for his self, because ain't no way you would have took that leap. But, of course, I ain't known you for more than an hour, so only God knows what goes through your mind. You sho look like a real sharp girl though."

"Lisa, can you please just whip my hair? Dang. I ain't come in here for y'all to try and dissect me. I love my man. He's my best half. He meets me halfway, and then some. He's my Adam and I am his rib. That's just that."

The high yellow woman laughed. "Girl, show me his picture. I bet he fine as hell."

"Yeah, give up the goods," Lisa encouraged, nudging me.

The bells clanged on the door. Jazzy stepped into the salon with her cellphone glued to her ear, talking all sultry into it. All of the females in the salon turned to look her over. She was fitted in a tight black and white Prada pants suit, over black red-bottoms. "Hey, June." She waved to the light-skinned female.

"Hey you, it's about time you got here. I was about to fill your seat in thirty more minutes, with one of my clients that's looking to be squeezed in. Whenever you book an appointment when you're in town you're always late." June turned up her nose.

"Girl, hush. Huh." She handed her a hundred-dollar-bill. "You know I always do you right. Now handle your bidness. I need the usual." She placed her phone into her purse and set it in her lap. "What you hens in here clucking about anyway?"

June smacked her lips. "Uh-huh." She draped a cover around Jazzy's neck and turned on the sink. "Your lil bribes ain't gon always suffice. You better work on being on time."

"Girl, hush." Jazzy rolled her eyes. "What was y'all talking about?" She acted as if she didn't even see me sitting four chairs over from her. Since she didn't speak, I didn't either.

"We was trying to get Miss Lady here to show us a picture of this man she done married, all young and stuff. I know he gots to be a sight to see for a pretty girl such as herself to marry him so young. Or, he gots to be rich. Either way, I wanna see what he look like. Come on, girl, let me see."

"Yeah, show us what you working wit," June said, running her fingers through Jazzy's hair.

"I can vouch that he fine," Jazzy offered.

The shop got quiet. There were five beauticians all together working on their clients and every last one of them stopped and looked toward Jazzy. I felt my temper rising.

"Girl, how you know that?" June asked, with her hand on her hip.

"Aw, we all know each other. Besides, I know him from back in the day. He used to talk to one of my girls, and we were all acquainted with each other in one way or the other."

Lisa let out a gasp of air. "Honey, so y'all know each other?" She asked this question looking down at me.

I was trying to remain calm. My heart was pounding in my chest. "Yeah, I know her, but it ain't all what she making it out to be. She's a distant friend. That's all." I glanced at her from the corners of my eyes. My head was halfway covered with the relaxer. Had it not been, I would have been all over Jazzy's ass for her insinuations. What the fuck did she mean, she knew him from back in the day? Did her and Bentley share a past he'd not let me in on? And if that was the case, what could his reason be for doing so? I thought that our bond was deeper than that? Had they screwed around since we'd been down in Miami? My brain got to going into overdrive. Suddenly, I needed to confront Bentley. Needed to find out what was going on between those two.

Jazzy held out her phone. "Here he go right here, all six feet of his fine ass."

The women rushed around her phone. They ooo-ed and ahh-ed, and gave each other high fives, agreeing on how fine Bentley was. This vexed me so bad that I started to shake.

Lisa came back over and took ahold of my hair and started to apply more of the relaxer to it. "Girl, I see why you married that man, he's fine."

"Mmm-hmm," June agreed. "He look like a younger, sexier version of Idris Elba. I would have married his ass too. Construction worker at that? That means that he's good with his hands. That's a manly man. Lord knows those are rare."

"Tell me about it." Lisa snickered. "These men nowadays are so feminine. Clothes tighter than ours. And wear more make-up then we do. I miss the days when there were hardcore men, men that could handle a woman with care. But, you done found you a man that's a hard worker and good with his hands. You're blessed, especially if he treat you right."

"That ain't all he good wit," Jazzy said, just above a whisper.

Once again the entire shop stopped what they were doing to look her over. She sat in the chair getting her hair shampooed, with a meek smile on her face. I could tell she was saying things to get under my skin, and as much as I hated to admit it, she was.

"Girl, what you mean by that?" June asked, pursing her lips.

"Yeah, spill that tea," said another heavy set beautician.

I held my silence. Inside my blood was boiling like Ramen Noodles on a stove that was turned up too high. I kept seeing images of me blowing her head off her shoulders. The sight was the only thing that calmed me down to a certain degree internally.

"Well?" Lisa pushed.

"Let's just say that I know he's a savage when it comes to that bedroom. I'm talking the truth. He lasts way more than the average five minutes of most niggas. And, he strapped like an elephant. But, that's all I'ma say, 'cause it is her husband and all. I don't want to be disrespectful."

"Sound like you being a ho," Lisa snickered and continued relaxing my hair.

"Girl, ain't you gon say anything? She over here promoting your man more than a Facebook ad and you ain't said not a word. Umph! You better than me. I'da chased her ass out of here with a pair of these scissors," said a Puerto Rican beautician.

I saw red. Saw Jazzy's murder, her funeral and me smiling in the front pew. I didn't want to get into a shouting match with a female over my man. That seemed counterproductive to me. I had to approach Bentley about the situation first. Read him and go from there. If he said the wrong thing, that would get Jazzy screwed over. I was thinking a couple hot ones to her pretty face oughta do the trick.

"Yeah, baby, ain't you got nothing to say?" Lisa asked.

"Nope. I'm good. Just whip my hair, girl. Do your thing and I'll make sure I take care of you." I closed my eyes and Bentley's image came into my mind's eye, shirtless. He was fine, but he belonged to me. I would approach him after I did some digging. I wasn't gon play 'bout mine. Jazzy would find that out in due time.

Chapter 8
Bentley

"Kid, what the fuck we doing in Jacksonville, son? You ain't say nothing about traveling out of Miami." I took a strong pull off of the Miami Loud, and inhaled the ganja deeply. I was so high that my eyes were lower than the sole on the bottom of a shoe. But, I was focused and in my mode, ready to handle bidness.

"Yo, Dunn, I never told you we weren't leaving Miami either. We gotta go where the money is. These Haitians are spread out all over the state, bruh. They do their dirt in Miami and be having all types of duck-offs in surrounding cities. That's where we gotta go to hit they ass. Catch 'em slipping with they people and whatnot. Nah mean?" He sniffed loudly and pulled his nose. Before we loaded into his truck, I'd watched him toot about two grams of boy, and down a half-bottle of lean. He had to be fucked up. I worried about his impairment. Hoped he could handle business under the influence.

"I mean, it is what it is. The payout is fifty gees no matter what, right?" I needed to confirm that for the tenth time on this trip alone.

Lethal laughed. "Yeah nigga, damn. You done asked me that a million times. No matter what, you getting fifty gees for this move. If we come up on anything else, that's an added benefit. But that fifty is what's good. Why, you don't trust the god or something?" He adjusted the MAC-11 that was on his lap. It had a blue bandana around the handle.

I sat back in my seat and nodded my head to the Lox album he was banging out of his speakers. "It ain't got nothin to do wit trust, bruh. I just needed to make sure that number was out there, and it was agreed to. The more times I reiterate that and it's confirmed is better for me. That's what it is. This ain't my first time getting down outta state wit a nigga. A few times them numbers ain't add up and that was a cause for concern later on. You feel me?"

"Well, it ain't nothin' like that gon happen this time. I already got our bags. I just ain't hit you wit that cash yet. Want us to handle our bidness first. It's all love. This one is sweet, we're going under the cover of a high stakes craps game. There's only a few choice cats that have been invited. And we're two of them. The nigga that's hosting the game is plugged with Damo. He already know what the deal is, so halfway through the game he gon bounce and we gon take care of everybody that's left around the table. Badda bing, badda boom. It's as simple as that. You wit me?"

"Long as that paper one hunnit, I'm wit you. That's fa sho." I looked out of the window at the cars that were flying by us, headed down the interstate.

"Yo, I see why you rocking wit Jade so hard too. Shorty fine as hell. Had I come across something that cold, I would have cuffed it too. I don't know about the whole wife thing though. I love fucking all kinds of different pussies, so that would be a stretch for me. But then again, I already know you fuckin' other hoes, ain't you?" He laughed, then glanced over at me.

"Nall, son, I don't need to. I got everything I need right there in her. Can't no other female do the things she do for me. My rib more than one hunnit. Word up."

"That's what's up. I know Jazzy feeling you like a mafucka though. The other night when I was waxing that ass, this bitch had the nerve to call out your name when she came. Ain't that fucked up?"

66

"For you. I ain't never fucked no bitch and she called out another nigga name. Had that happened, I would have made her get the fuck out of my bed like ASAP. Sound like you hit problems, kid. Might have to check ya dame in." I wondered what was Jazzy's problem? Why was she lusting after me so hard? What had Keri told her? Then I'd slipped up and got hard in front of her, that couldn't help matters any. Damn, I was slipping. I had to be extra careful around her.

"I don't be studding shorty like that. We been fucking for a few years now and it ain't nothin serious. She got her purposes, and that's just that. Beyond those measures, I just don't care. Long as I can fuck when I want to. She got a crazy shot between her legs too. A nigga can never get enough of that. Before you bounce to Havana, I'll bet you a gee you wind up hitting that shit. Watch."

I smacked my lips. "Yo, you might as well hand that band over right now. She bad and all of that shit, but ain't no bitch bad enough to make me step out on my Jade. That ain't happening right there, trust me on that."

Lethal shook his head. "Jade is bad though. I can see why you feel like you feel. She got an ass on her that don't quit. And that whole slightly bow-legged thing is most definitely working for her. Yeah, I can see what you see."

I mugged this nigga and was seconds away from moving on his ass. I already knew my wife was bad. I didn't need no nigga telling how bad she was. That only pissed me off, especially because I could really tell he was feeling her. "Yo, let's focus back on this mission, Dunn. That shit you talking about over there ain't healthy for neither one of us." I felt my heart pounding like crazy. I was seconds away from going off of the deep end over Jade. She belonged to me. I felt like this nigga was overstepping all kinds of bounds.

"Yo, what I say?" he asked, looking offended.

"I don't play about my rib. Keep them comments and thoughts to yourself. That's all I'ma tell you. Now, what's good? How far are we away from our destination?"

He was quiet for about a full minute. Scoffed, and looked over at me. "Bout thirty more minutes cuz. That cool wit you?"

I nodded. "Yop." Leaned forward and turned the Lox album all the way up, before laying back and getting my mind together for what was to take place.

***

An hour later, I stood at the head of the casino-like table with the dice in my hand, shaking them. There were four other men present besides me and Lethal. All of them had thick and dusty looking dread locks and spoke broken English. When they communicated amongst themselves, they spoke in a foreign language that I could understand. That bothered me because when I was in a room with men I liked to know what was being discussed, especially when it came to a move like the one we were about to pull.

Lethal had given me five thousand dollars to shoot craps with before we were let inside the large house. The buy-in was a thousand dollars, and all fades were no less than a hundred. I'd been shooting for five minutes and already I had a pot of ten thousand sitting in front of me. While shooting, I took my time to size up each man. They all looked over thirty, drunk, and high. I could also see the butts of their guns poking out of their shirts. All four were a bit slim. Their eyes were bloodshot.

I blew into my fist and rolled the dice again on to the carpet covered pit that the men stood around with hundred-dollar-bills in their hands. The dice stopped at the far end of the table, adding up to the number six, a four and a two.

"Yo, that's my mans. I say he six-eight for a gee," Lethal offered to the Haitian standing next to him.

The man counted out ten, one-hundred-dollar-bills and dropped them on the table. "I fade you on the six-eight bet, and for another thousand I say he can't straight six for the pot." He was basically saying he didn't think I could win the pot by rolling a straight six, and also that I would roll either a seven, eleven, snake eyes, twelve, or three before I rolled a six or a three. All craps killed a six-eight side bet. All of the odds were against me in this bet, but I was good with those dice. Had been since I was a youngin' back in Red Hook.

Letha dropped another stack and moved their money to the side. "You ain't said nothing but a word. Cuz got this."

The man who'd let us inside the house cleared his throat. "Any more bets? Anybody?" he questioned, looking from man to man. When it seemed that nobody else wanted in, he nodded. "Alright then, proceed, lil brother. Let's see what you got. He was the only bald man at the table. Sweat glistened on the top of his head and slid down the side of his face.

I stacked the dice, picked them up and shook them hard before rolling them across the table. They bounded off the far end and stopped to a halt on the number nine, a five and a four.

The man that had let us into the house and introduced us as friends of his scooped them and rolled them back to me. "Nine. The point is six. No more bets."

I shook the dice and blew into my fist again. Rolled them down the table and they landed on double fours. Lethal picked up his gee from the six-eight bet, being that I'd hit one of the two numbers I was supposed to. The Haitian to the left of him threw down another stack and motioned for me to continue. Lethal faded him again by leaving a gee in place from the side pile they'd place the original bet on.

"Yo kid, stop playin wit them, gon 'head and make that happen." He laughed and winked at me.

The man that had let us inside of the house caught our signal and backed out of the game room. "I'll be back, gentlemen, my stomach is getting the best of me," he said, holding his butt and disappearing from the room.

"Fuck him. Shoot, Zoe. Shoot," the man to the left of Lethal hollered. He sounded impatient, and irritated.

"Yeah, shoot cuz." Lethal curled his lip and took a minor step back that only I seemed to peep. Husband went behind him.

I threw the dice as hard as I could. They rolled hard. One of them flew off of the table and onto the floor. The Haitians turned to see where the dice went.

As soon as their attention was diverted, I came out of my shirt with two forty .40 Glocks. The hammers already cocked, I aimed at the one I'd been gambling with and pulled the trigger three times. *Boom. Boom. Boom.* The shots sent him flying backwards with big holes in his face.

Lethal went on a rampage, aiming and shooting, chopping down the men before they could get out their own weapons to return fire. He aimed for their heads. His shots were precise, dropping them one by one.

I gathered up the money and stuffed my pockets as best I could, then followed behind him as we made our way from the bottom of the house. When we got upstairs, the man from before was standing in the kitchen, holding a book bag in his hand. He handed it to Lethal. "Here, boy. Now hit me right here. Hurry up." He pointed to his shoulder. "Make it look good."

Lethal stepped back and slammed his banger to his neck and pulled the trigger, splashing him. The act caught me completely off guard. So much so, that I jumped backwards. "Punk ass nigga. Ain't no way I'm leaving you to tell shit. Let's go, cuz."

T.J. & Jelissa

Chapter 9
Jade

I tossed and turned in the bed for the fifth night in a row. It had been five days since Jazzy had said the things she did about Bentley inside the beauty salon, and they were still getting the better of me. I'd had yet to bring them to his attention, because I'd decided to take a different approach. Whenever we were in the same room with her, I simply watched his eyes. Paid attention to how he followed her whenever she got up or sat down and crossed her big legs. She made a habit of serving him in my presence, and whenever it looked like he was in need of anything, she took it upon herself to make sure that he got it. Her skirts appeared shorter whenever we were around, her pants tighter. I was so frustrated by the situation I didn't know what to do. Lethal's cousin was the key to us making it out of the United States. I didn't want to screw things up by going at his broad with my jealous emotions. But, holding my tongue was getting the best of me. It was even making it hard for me to eat and I knew it was damaging for our child. I had to get it together, and soon.

Bentley slid into the bed at about three o'clock this morning. Kissed the back of my neck, then sucked on the side of it. "Jade," he whispered, "Baby, are you asleep?" kissing my neck.

I was about to lie there and ignore him. I couldn't help but to remember how his eyes had followed Jazzy around the room. I wondered if he was getting tired of me. The same ol' kitty. If that natural male part of him was starting to yearn for another female, that worried me. "Yeah, baby. I'm awake. Did you just get in?" I asked this question, already knowing the answer to it.

"Yeah, I had to take care of something wit Lethal, but it's good now." Husband slid around until he was rubbing my stomach. "Baby, every time I rub this stomach, it make me feel some type of way." He sucked my neck again and licked all over it. "I love you so much, Jade. Do you know that?" His fingers slipped past the hem of my panties. Traveled downward. He cupped my mound, and ran a finger in between the lips, pulled it out and sucked it clean.

"I love you too, Bentley. Now go to sleep. I'm not in the mood right now." Once again, I was having thoughts about Jazzy and what he might have been doing before he slid in the bed with me altogether. Maybe I was no longer enough, with my stomach beginning to poke out, and my attitude getting worse.

"Yo, it's good, boo. I just wanna eat my pussy for a lil while. I need to have you on my tongue so I can sleep. You already know I'm obsessed with your taste. Have been since the beginning. So, just let me do my thing, ma. I'll put you back to sleep." He sank low in the bed and got behind me. Raised my gown and kissed all over my round backside. Then his face was in my crack. His tongue swiped at my box, sending shivers through me. My juices began to form.

"Stop, baby. I ain't feeling you right now. Damn. Don't make me mule kick you." I didn't mean to be sound so evil, but I was hurting. This bitch was all under my skin and I felt that a part of him wanted her.

He sat up. "Fuck is wrong wit you?" Flicked on the lamp and got out of the bed.

Now, I sat up. "Don't be cursing at me. You know I don't like when you speak unseasoned to me."

"Well, it's kind of hard to do that. I come in the room from bussing my ass out there in those streets, yearning to taste my woman's pussy and here you are, acting all stuck up and shit. What's your problem?"

I glared at him. "Bentley, if you curse at me one more time, you and I are about to tear this room up. Speak to me as if I am your wife. Not one of them bitches in the street. That's my last time telling you that." I got up and walked into the bathroom. Gargled some mouthwash and spit it out, fuming. Who was he to talk to me in such a way? Was it because he was fucking somebody else? Jazzy, for that matter? Yeah, I bet.

He stepped into the bathroom and stood behind me. "Yo, baby, I'm sorry. You're right. I know I gotta come at you better than that. You're my wife. The love of my life. I love you, boo" He leaned in to kiss my cheek.

I jerked away from him and stepped back into the bedroom. I didn't feel right with his lips touching me. Not until I found out if he and Jazzy had anything going on behind my back. My mother had always told me the eyes were windows to the soul. If that was the case, his windows were following Jazzy all around the room the last time all of us had been together. That meant his soul yearned for another woman. Not me.

"Jade, what is the matter? Talk to me before I snap the hell out. Speak!" He followed me into the bedroom. Took his shirt off and threw it on the bed. His abs were prominent as he inhaled and exhaled angrily.

I squirted lotion into my hands and rubbed it in, sitting on the edge of the bed. "Just tired of this stuff, Bentley. Tired. It's as simple as that."

"Of what, Jade? Talk to me. What's good? I need to know?" He came and knelt in front of me, tried to take ahold of my hand.

I yanked it away again. "Don't touch me, Bentley. I don't know where your hands have been."

He stood up. "My hands? Where they been?" He sucked his teeth. "On a muthafuckin' pistol, so I can provide for me and you to make it so we ain't gotta worry about shit when we leave this bitch. "Matter fact," he said, bounced up and opened the closet door. Knelt down and started to throw shoe boxes out of it.

"What are you doing?" I hollered.

"Shut up, Jade, damn. You gon see."

"You shut up."

There was a bunch of rambling in the closet, and then he backed out of it with a duffle bag in his hand. "Better watch yo mouth. Fuck you mean shut up. I'm the head. You shut up and pay attention." He slung the bag on the bed and unzipped it.

"Bentley, check yo self nigga fa real. You might be the head, but I'm still a queen. Don't forget that." I rolled my eyes at him.

"Shut up and look at this." He turned the bag over and dumped it out. Stacks and stacks of cash with rubber bands holding them together fell out of it. There was so much money inside of it that it covered from the middle of the bed on down. "You see this shit? This is two hundred and seventy-five thousand dollars. This is from hitting a few moves with that nigga Lethal. I been all over Florida, and we got a few more to go. So, you wanna know where my hands have been, they been deep in the shit that's getting us right." He started to pack the bag again. "What's your problem anyway?"

I exhaled loudly. "Nothing, baby. Nothing at all, I was just bugging for a minute. I'm sorry." I walked over to him and opened my arms. "You forgive me?"

He pursed his lips. This made his dimples appear deeply on each cheek. "Yo, you having crazy mood swings, goddess. You got me walking on eggshells. We gotta get on the same page, or that's gon be damaging for us. What's wrong?"

"Do you forgive me or not?" Now, I was starting to feel a bit emotional.

He pulled me to him and wrapped me in his big arms. "Of course, I forgive you, Jade. You're my baby. There is nothing you could ever do that I couldn't forgive. This is us, baby. We are one." He kissed my forehead and held me for a few minutes. He made me feel so secure protected, so warm, so sheltered. He let me go, and moved my hair out of my face, and tucked it behind my ear. "You're so beautiful, baby. I wanna taste you so bad. But, I'll wait. It's good." Kissed my forehead again and replaced the duffle bag inside of the closet.

I stood there shifting my weight from one foot on to the next. I didn't want together into any argument with my man, but my insecurities were getting the better of me. "Bentley, baby, can you be honest with me for a minute? Please?"

He came out of the closet after stacking the shoe boxes neatly as they had been before. Stood up and faced me. "You already know I will. What's up, baby? Talk to me."

I took his hand and led him to the bed. We sat, and then I had to sit there for a minute trying to gather my thoughts, before I said the wrong thing. I just needed a few reassurances. I was drowning, and I didn't know why. I just needed to hear a few answers from him. I exhaled with my jaws full of air. "Baby, we down here in Miami for a few weeks now. I can't help but to notice that everywhere I look is a beautiful woman, and most of the times that you are with me they are eyeing you. So, I guess my question to you is, how long will it be before you wind up messing around on me if you haven't done it already? Be honest?"

He slid off of the bed and ran his hand over his face. Walked toward the closet, stopped and looked back at me. "That's what's been bothering you? Really? That's the reason why I ain't got yo lil ass folded up right now, drinking them juices?"

"Don't overreact, Bentley, just tell me the truth. That's all I wanna know."

"Baby, fuck these hoes! I don't care about them. We from New York, it's pretty bitches everywhere just like it is down here."

"Wow, so you have noticed?"

"Yeah, I'm a man, of course I've noticed. But, it still stands, fuck them hoes. I love you. Ain't nobody got shit on my wife! Yo, when I'm out there I'm trying to make it happen for us, I ain't standing around looking at no bitch, or trying to fuck wit 'em on no level. My loyalty to you, my Rib, is first and most important. Our bond is deeper than the looks of one of these broads out here. Come on now." He frowned and shook his head.

I lowered mine. "Yeah, well I'm gaining weight. My stomach about to be poking out in a minute and then these stupid scars all over my back. Pretty soon them "bitches" gon' start to look real good and then what. Huh?"

"Then nothing!" He stepped in front of me and pulled me up. "Yo, this is us. I'd kill for you Jade. I'll body anything over or about you. You've saved my life not once but twice. I'd be dead in the ground had it not been for you. So don't never think that just because a bitch look some type of way that they could ever be on your level. You are my heart, and my soul. I'd ride for you. You understand that?" He brushed my hair out of my face again.

"Yeah, I do. I'm just freaking out is all. I'm thinking about what this baby is going to do to my body, and the long term effect of looking like that when all of these broads sniffing around you. I don't wanna have to kill yo ass and raise this baby on my own, but if I had too I will." I meant every word of that too. I would murder Bentley in a heartbeat if he ever thought that he was going to be able to leave me for some prettier female with an easier situation. The response that his pictures had gotten from the females in the beauty shop was bothering me nearly a week later. Why Jazzy had pics of him in her phone was still an issue that I wanted to address. I saw myself getting even with her real soon.

"Baby, your body is going to change. You are about to bring life into this world. Our life. A little me and you. In order for that to happen your body has to change in a way for you to accommodate our baby. That's a gift. But just because your body changes does not mean that my love for you will as well. I love you and am obsessed with everything about my Queen. You ain't got nothing to worry about. I'ma be the best man for you, until my last breath. That's on our lil one." He pulled me into his embrace again and hugged me tight.

"I just get insecure sometimes, baby. I'ma get stronger. These emotions, our situation, the way these broads be jocking you. It's just crazy. I gotta get ahold of myself. That's all, baby." I kissed his lips. In the back of my mind, I wanted to ask him about his feelings toward Jazzy. Not his emotional feelings, but his lustful ones. I wanted to dive deeper into their past to find out just how acquainted they'd actually been. But I didn't want us to argue further couldn't stand for us to be in a bad space, not while my emotions were all out of whack. I loved my husband, and I trusted him. I had to. We were all we had.

"Baby, I take it you still ain't about to let me taste that thang tonight, huh?" he asked, laughing a lil bit.

"Baby, to be honest, I just want you to hold me tonight. Hold me and keep telling me how much you love and desire me. Tell me you feel blessed to be my husband. That you are honored we are having a baby together. Can you do that?"

He picked me up. My thighs wrapped around his body. He looked into my eyes, then kissed my lips. "Of course, I can, ma. You're my baby."

And that's just what he did for the whole night through.

Chapter 10
Bentley

Lethal took a long swallow from the Pink Sprit draining its contents, then tossed the empty bottle into the garbage can that was on the side of the couch in his living room. Wiped his mouth with the back of his hand, and burped loudly, hitting himself on the chest with a sideways closed fist. "Damn," he muttered.

Jazzy walked into the living room in a pair of booty shorts that were way too small for her. Her chocolate thighs jiggled with each step she took, before she dropped a Batman book bag into Lethal's lap. Eyed me, licked her lips and walked back into the room, closing the door.

Lethal grabbed the book bag, and unzipped it. Dug his hand inside of it and pulled out three stacks of cash that had rubber bands around them, tossed them across the living room to me. "Huh, bruh, that's thirty bands right there. You'll get the other twenty after we get back from Tallahassee tomorrow night, and I might have something else for you too. That just depends on how things go when we get down here," he added.

I thumbed through the money with a blunt hanging from my lip. The smoke was so potent that it burned my left eye. After eyeing about three hundred one-hundred-dollar bills, I tucked the cash away. "Yo, before you even tell me 'bout this lil move over in Tallahassee, it's been three months, bruh, and we still don't know what's good wit yo cousin, man. Them people got bounties on me and my wife's head for a million apiece, and they steady raising money through this go fund me shit. It's getting hotter and hotter for us to be in Miami, or these states period. We gotta get a move on. What's the latest word?"

Lethal closed his eyes and ran his hand over his face. "Man, I'm fucked up. Think I put too much in that Sprite." He yawned and stretched his arms over his head. "He just beat two of them cases over there and got one left. That one shouldn't take more than a few weeks. So unfortunately, we gon have to be patent, but in the meantime, we can keep hitting these licks and get our money right. That way when he does break free of that chaos he got going on there, you and your woman a be loaded up. That money a go a long way in Havana, trust me on that." He yawned again and leaned all the way back.

"That's if we ever get to that bitch. Damn, nigga. It feel like you selling me a pipe dream a somethin'. Word up. I been hearing about yo cousin ever since I been, shit since before we left Jersey and I ain't seen or heard from that nigga yet. Bruh, what's really good?" I stood up and peered down at him.

"This Tallahassee move gon set us on the right foot. We about to ex a few of the bosses that's major in that whole Zoe thing. I don't know the internal politics like that, but I do know that once we cap these clowns, we'll open up an avenue for some serious cash that flows from there, all the way back down to here in Miami. That's why we gotta make some serious noise. I'm thinking fifty gees is a given, but if we really hit the right ones I'ma make sure I add another ten on top of that. How that sound to you?"

I played with the hairs on my chin. I was lost in deep thought. Sixty gees sounded real good. I could add it to the stash that me and Jade had already accrued and that would push us just past three hundred thousand. It was more money than I had seen in my entire life. I expected to do a lot with it once we got to our next destination across the water in Havana, Cuba. "That sound real good, but at the same time, if ya cousin ain't gon be able to make this shit happen for me and my wife, then maybe he can call in a favor or something. Better yet, maybe you know somebody else that get down with the whole people smuggling thing? Do you?"

His head was laid all the way back on the couch. Mouth wide open, snoring. The bag of money still opened on his lap. He was snoring louder and louder, irritating me. I felt like punching his ass right in the throat.

Jazzy came out of the room, shaking her head. "Don't make no damn sense. That's why I don't fuck with that shit myself. All it do is make you feel sleepy all day. Then he's on that China white. It's just too much. Ugh." She rolled her eyes and took the bag from his lap. "Don't worry Bentley, I can out you up on game about this Tallahassee move, after all I'ma be the one that'll be doing most of the work, by the time y'all get there the job will be half over. Hold on let me put this back." She walked off with her shorts all in her ass.

I glanced over to Lethal. He scratched at his neck, snorted loudly before continuing to snore. I couldn't wait to shake this nigga. To me he was too sloppy. He was always high or drunk, and I didn't like operating under those terms. I felt a man needed a clear head at times when he was involved in the kind of lifestyle we were in, whereas Lethal had a problem. He was always impaired in some kind of way.

Jazzy came back into the living room and mugged the sleeping Lethal, then looked up at me. "Come on, let's go in here so we can talk. He snoring all loud and shit. It's annoying." She waved me to follow her.

I looked back at Lethal one good time and shook my head in disgust before I followed Jazzy into the back room, where she sat on the bed, with her phone in her hand.

"Close that door too," she ordered.

I did. "Yo, what's this you talking about you gon be doing most of the work? Kid, ain't said nothin' to me about none of that."

"He also ain't told you that his so-called cousin is my actual brother, and that he gon be in that jam for at least another three months. The only way y'all getting out of this country anytime soon is through me. I done already cast my net to find a good human smuggler for y'all, it won't be long until I'm hit back. I'm on top of it. But, when it comes to Lethal, you can't believe everything that comes out of his mouth. He exaggerates a bit because he's always fucked up on some thing or the other. I mean, he means well. But I run this shit. I'm the brains, and he's the brawn. Florida is my state. I been back and forth since I was a little girl. I know all of my brother's connects. He trusts me more than he trusts anybody else in this world." She picked up a blunt from the ashtray on the nightstand and set fire to it, took three quick puffs, inhaling the smoke deeply.

I stood there perplexed. Scratched my head, trying to make some sense of what she was telling me. "Yo, so what the fuck he got going on in the Dominican Republic anyway?" I wanted to know.

"First of all, he isn't in the Dominican Republic, he's jammed up in Port Au Prince, Haiti. He beat two of the three murders he was charged with, and on the way to beating the third. The reason you guys having been knocking off Haitians left and right, is because they all have something to do with my brother's cases. Well, that and their demise is crucial so we can get the right amount of footing down here." She dumped the ashes from her blunt and crossed her thick thighs. Took another puff with her right eye slightly closed, because of the smoke wafting from her blunt.

"Footing? What you mean?"

"Oh, Lethal didn't tell you?" She laughed, "It figures. Anyway, he's trying to bring Camden to the three-oh-five. He wants to build a fast-money-getting army of savages in which he sits atop the throne of. That's why he's running back and forth to Camden nearly twice a week every week. I'm surprised he didn't tell you all of that."

"Shid, why are you telling me so much? I thought you was loyal to the homie and all of that shit?"

"I'm loyal to me first, and then my brother, Damo. That's it. I fuck wit Lethal because he's an animal, and we've been getting rich together. But, he doesn't own me. The reason why I'm telling you what's good is because number one, I like you. Then number two, you have the right to know what you're getting into. You got a whole ass pregnant girl to worry about, and you're putting your life on the line every time you go up against those Haitians. I should know because I am Haitian, and some of the people we're putting down is of my bloodline. They are animals, just like you and Lethal. That's why on this next mission, I'm going to take the lead. I'm going under the guise of a stripper. You guys will be invading a bachelor party. Three of the targets will be there. You'll have to annihilate them, and that'll be that. Any questions?"

"Yo, something ain't right. I need to get these numbers in order. How much is this nigga really getting paid for each move?"

"Fifty gees a head. If y'all hit three niggas in one room and they have anything to do wit my brother's case that's one fifty. Knowing Lethal, he'll probably give you a third, then he'll give a third to me and keep the rest. He ain't been playing you when it comes to your money if that's what you're worried about."

"Why the fuck is he giving you a third if you ain't have nothing to do with the missions? That basically mean y'all are keeping sixty-six percent of all profits. That ain't what's good. If I'm bussing my gun, I should get the same amount he do. Everything should be spilt fifty-fifty."

She scoffed. "Nall, it don't go like that. You see, Damo put the moves in circulation, then we buss them. The third of the cash I get actually goes back to my brother for lawyer fees, and some other things that he needs help with while he's in the land of the Haitians. Their jails are way different from the ones we're used to in the states. Over there, if your family don't provide it you ain't getting it. Three meals a day there isn't guaranteed. It's crazy."

"So, he's the one that set up all of the moves. We buss them, and on goes the saga, huh?"

She nodded. "Yep. One hand washes the other."

"Well, at least I know what's good. I'm down for this Tallahassee one, just make sure that I get my bread and I ain't gone have a problem handling my biz. Make sure you keep working on getting us up out of this country though. That is most important."

She set the blunt in the ashtray. "I got you, Bentley. Just keep doing what you are and when the time is right, you and Jade a be up out of here. Okay?" She smiled and sucked her bottom lip into her mouth.

"Aiight. Well, I'ma get on over here and see what's good wit my baby. I'll holler at y'all in a few hours or so." I grabbed ahold of the door handle.

She jumped from the bed so fast and pushed it back closed before I could open it. "Wait a minute." She said, looking up at me. Her face was inches away from my own.

86

"What's good Jazzy?"

"Why are you so afraid of me? Every time you're in my presence it's like you don't know where to look, or what to do. Do I make you nervous because we share some of the same thoughts about each other?"

I smacked my lips. "Bitch, you don't know what the fuck going on in my head. Our thoughts ain't in synch. You got shit twisted. Watch out." I tried to peel her hand away from the door, but she pushed harder with all of her strength.

"Wait, Bentley, damn. Can you hear me out for a second?" she pleaded, struggling to keep the door closed.

I released her hand. "Hurry up, what's good?"

She looked into my eyes and trailed her hand over my chest, before I smacked it away. This made her take a few steps back. She looked hurt. "Look Bentley, I'm the key to you and her getting the fuck outta Miami, wit out them people moving in on y'all ass. I can make this shit happen in a matter of weeks, or a matter of months, it just depends on how nice y'all are to me, and by y'all I mean you." She stepped forward again and rested both hands on my chest.

"What's that supposed to mean, shorty?"

She rubbed all over my shoulders, then back down to my chest. "I just wanna see what all this is about one time. Need you to dick me down one time. That's all I ask. You do that and I swear, everything will be put in place for y'all to get out of here. But before that happens, you gotta let me ride this, Bentley." Her hand roamed down my stomach and cuffed my dick through my jeans. She squeezed it and gasped. "I knew you were hung, daddy." Her hands played all over my lower region, before she sank to her knees, unbuckling my belt and unbuttoning my pants so fast that before I knew it, they were both sliding down my thighs.

She squeezed my dick again through the material of my boxers. "I ain't heard no moaning over there in a few weeks. I usually hear that every night. Something ain't right, but it ain't my bidness." She sniffed me through my shorts and moaned. "Damn, I gotta taste this." She tried to pull it out of the boxers and I slapped her hand away.

"You right, it ain't yo bidness. So, stay in yo fuckin' lane. I already told you that if you trying to get some of this, you gon gave to holler at my wife and she ain't going for it, so good luck wit that." I pulled up my pants and straightened my clothes. Once again, my dick was rock hard from fucking wit Jazzy. I had to stay away from his bitch or she was gon get me in a world of trouble.

Jazzy stood up with her hand running up and down her stomach.

"Damn, why are you acting so funny, Bentley? Keri already told me how you get down. You don't love them hoes like that, so why you fronting?"

I made sure I was all the way straight. "Shorty, you need to get ahold of yourself. I ain't fucking wit you like that. Jade is my heart. Let's just stick to this bidness and keep everything professional. Nah mean?"

She shook her head. "Fuck that. You gon fuck me. I don't care what you talking about. I'ma stay in my lane for now, but don't think that I'm about to reach far and wide for you when you can't even lay me down. Like we said before, one hand washes the other." She crawled on the bed and walked across it on her knees, pulled the material of the shorts as hard as she could. That big ass was all in the air, the booty shorts barely present in her crack.

My piece got to throbbing again as I watched her lips appear through the fabric. I already knew what I would do to her if I got on that shit, but I couldn't. My heart was with Jade. I shook my head and opened the bedroom door, stepped out into the living room.

Lethal was at the side door of the apartment with it open. He was saying something, saw me and pointed. "There go Bentley right there."

I looked past him to Jade and my eyes got as big as saucers.

T.J. & Jelissa

Chapter 11
Jade

"For the last time, Bentley, what the fuck was you doing over there in the room with that bitch, with the door closed at that? Huh?"

He sat on the couch with his head hung low. "Ma, my word. All me and the bitch was doing was talking bidness. She explained everything to me that that fool Lethal been slacking on. I got a way better understanding now about everything. It's good."

I walked over to him, and slapped him so hard, I felt bad after I did it. He fell to one knee. "What the fuck kind of business are you discussing with this bitch that you need to be in a closed room discussing? You think I'm stupid or somethin'? Do you?"

He stayed on one knee holding his face. Slowly stood up and laughed. "Yo, I love you, boo, but keep yo muthafuckin' hands to yourself. You got my kid inside of you, so I ain't gon return what you just sent to me. But, don't touch me no more. On everything." He wiped his mouth. I saw I'd split it enough to cause blood.

"I ain't worried about you doing nothing to me, Bentley. That's the last thing I'm worried about! Now, answer my fuckin' question?"

He started to pace. "Yo, we need to get back in that Bible. Your mouth been getting just as foul as mine lately, and everything you say, our shorty can hear that stuff now. Yo, dude was sleeping in the living room and shorty wanted to pull my coat to some thangs he ain't want me to know. That shit ain't take more than five minutes."

"Yousa five-minute lie! I was standing there talking to Lethal longer than that. Ooo, I swear to God. Did you fuck that bitch? Huh?" I walked up on him ready to strike again. My temper was at an all-time high. Not only was I pissed because of him being alone in the room with Jazzy, but he couldn't look me in the eyes. That told me he was lying to me. There had to be something going on between the two of them, and I wanted to know.

He backed away and held up his hands in preparation of me trying to strike him. "Yo, why are you wilin' right now? Ain't shit happen. You acting like you don't trust me and shit. After all we been through, you don't trust me?" He looked offended.

"Nigga I don't trust her. Plus I ain't been feeling too good so we ain't did our thing in more than a week. Ain't no telling how your nature is calling out. I already know you got a problem with controlling your libido. If you ain't getting it from me, ain't no telling what you doing wit her. You bet not have done shit wit her." I swung as hard as I could, trying to smack his head off.

He blocked it and jumped back. "Chill yo ass out, Jade! Fuck. You know I don't like nobody getting at me like you are. Now, please baby, stop trying to hit me in my shit. Damn. You know I'd never get down on you like that. I love yo ass way too much."

"You know what, I ain't finna do this, Bentley. I got a trick for this bitch." I rushed out of the living room and into our bedroom. Knelt down and pulled the Steve Madden show box from under the bed, then took the seventeen-shot Glock out of it. Slammed a clip into the handle, and cocked it back. I was about to take care of this Jazzy bitch once and for all. I was tired of playing games with her black ass. Every time I looked up, she was sniffing up my man or jocking him in some way, making nonchalant comments that were directed at me. I'd had enough. My stomach was feeling funny. I felt nauseous and had been feeling that way for the last week, and because me and Bentley had not been intimate. That worried me some but being that I was his wife the last thing I should of had to worry about was him cheating on me. It was supposed to be him and I. Us. I jumped up and made my way back into the living room.

He saw the gun in my hand and rushed in front of the door that split the two apartments. "Baby, what the fuck is you doing? Are you nuts? Go put that mafucka up."

I waved him off. "Move, Bentley. Move or I swear I'ma shoot through yo ass. I'ma show you what a bitch gon get from trying to play wit mine. Move!" I took a step back and aimed at him. I didn't know how close I was to actually bussing, but I was most definitely feeling some type of way.

He bucked his eyes, then lowered them into slits. "You gon shoot me, Jade? Really?"

"How come you ain't tell me you knew this bitch from back in the day? Why you ain't tell me y'all got history? She got pictures of you in her phone and stuff. How you think that make me feel?" My anger was getting the best of me, but I refused to cry. Not over him. Not over Jazzy. Not over nobody. I preferred to take that bitch off the face of this earth, and in this moment, him as well. I felt betrayed by the love of my life.

"Yo, put that fucking gun down, Jade. You acting real stupid right now, and it's pissing me off. Put that muthafucka down or pull the trigger. Those are your options. Word up."

I raised the gun, and got ready to shoot, but before I could the side door opened, and Bentley stumbled and fell on his back inside of Lethal's apartment. Lethal saw I had a gun in my hand and jumped back. "What the fuck going on over there?"

Jazzy ran from the couch to see what all of the ruckus was. She stood beside Lethal in a pair of booty shorts, and a wife beater that was way too tight for her. "Aw shit. That girl done finally lost her mind." She smiled and crossed her arms.

Bentley jumped up and rushed me. Picked me up. "Y'all close the door and quit being nosey. We good." He carried me down the hall toward the bedroom.

"Let me go, Bentley. Let me go, you hurting my stomach," I lied. I just wanted him to put me down.

He tossed me on the bed and snatched the gun out of my hand. Pulled the clip out of it and set it on the dresser. "Yo, you wilin' hard! What the fuck you trying to pull? You gon go at the bitch that's gon orchestrate us getting the fuck out of America and we got a million-dollar bounty apiece on our heads. Really?"

I was out of the bed with lightning speed, swinging wildly. My blows attacked his face. His chest. His hands. Any skin that I could get I was cool with. "I don't trust you and that bitch. I don't trust you and that bitch. I know you fucking her!" All the negative things that my mother had told me about men while I was growing up came rushing back to my mental. How they were cheaters and not to be trusted. How they were selfish, and abusive. That no matter what, they always found a way to hurt the woman they were with. If not right away, in time. The more I heard her voice in my head, the harder and longer I swung until finally I noticed that Bentley was no longer blocking the blows. He allowed for me to hit him anywhere that I wanted. After a couple shots to his face, I pulled back.

He stood up with his nose busted, a deep cut on his bottom lip. "This what you wanna do to me, Jade? Huh? This what's on your heart. Then go ahead. Go, baby. Go

94

until you get tired. Matter fact, huh pop this bitch." He slammed the clip back into the pistol and tried to hand it to me.

I moved it out of the way and fell to my knees. "I'm tired, Bentley. This life is too much. I'm so, so tired." Now tears streamed out of my eyes, and I hated myself for shedding tears in front of him after I'd acted so crazy. So unlike myself. My emotions were all over the place.

He knelt beside me and rubbed my back. "I love you, Jade. Damn. I'm tired too. You acting like you alone in this strug-gle. Me and you are fighting the same struggle. With the same goal in mind. We are all that we have. I ain't finna let nobody penetrate our bond. And you shouldn't either." He stopped and wiped blood from his lip. I felt horrible.

"I just need to know that you and her ain't creeping, Bent-ley. I swear to God I'll leave yo ass. I don't need you if you ain't gon be the man that you're supposed to be. I'll figure things out on my own. Trust and believe that." I threw his arm off of me and stood up.

He remained on his knees for two minutes longer, then stood up as well. "You belong to me, Jade. You're my baby. If you think you gon ever leave me, man, on my mother I'd take you out the game first. This is until the death. If there is no us, then there is no you or me. I'm letting you know that shit right now. So, quit talking all stupid or we can end both of our lives right now. Ours and our shorties'."

I glared at him and stepped in his face. "Don't tempt me, Bentley. The way I'm feeling right now, I might trick off and take you up on that offer. I swear to God, if I ever find out that you've been creeping wit that bitch, I'ma kill you and her. Now try me. Nigga, you created this monster, now you gotta deal with it. This is until the death, and that's just that."

He placed his forehead against mine. "That's yo word?"

"Nigga, that's my word."

***

Later that night, Bentley and I settled into the bathtub. I sat in between his legs and laid my head back against his muscular chest while he kissed the back of my neck. There were candles all around, with the light off in the bathroom. My phone was on top of the sink, and the sounds of R. Kelly's "Forevermore" were crooning out of it. The lyrics sounded so good to my soul. He ran the warm towel over my breasts.

"I'm sorry I snapped on you earlier, baby. I just been on edge lately. I don't like that Jazzy bitch. I know she got an agenda. But, I am sorry though. I should have allowed you to explain yourself before I put my hands on you."

He laughed. "You make me sound like a battered wife a somethin'. Ma, I ain't opposed to slapping the shit out of a female if she behaved like you did, but the man in me wouldn't allow for me to hit you. I love you way too much to ever hurt you like that. You gotta be smooth when you come at me though. You should already know I didn't fuck around on you. Come on, now."

"Yeah, I should of, but it's just that broad somethin' else. Baby?"

"Yeah, Jade."

"Do you find her attractive?"

"Come on, baby, let's not do this. You know that ain't gon get us nowhere but back into but back into another argument."

"So, that's a yes?"

"She straight, ma, but she ain't got nothing on you. You're all I need."

"Okay. Let's just say I wasn't in the picture, and she wanted to mess with you like she does right now, would you give her some play?" I didn't know why I was pressing the issue. Anything he said that fell in her favor wasn't going to do anything but piss me off further, but I guess I just wanted to know how honest my man would actually be with me.

"Yo, I can't imagine that, because you're my everything, so I'ma have to say no. Now, let's leave that whole subject alone, because it ain't healthy for us."

"Bentley, ain't nothing we have done this far been healthy for us. And, I don't know how much I believe you, but I'ma let this go. I meant what I said though. Now, you're telling me nothing ever happened in that room, right?"

"That's right. I wouldn't shit on you like that. You're my rib. That bitch don't mean nothing."

"Aiight, Bentley. Then we good. I said what I said. Now just hold me."

He laughed. "Shorty, it's crazy how you've turned into a female version of me. That killa shit is all up and through you. I love it, but at the same time it scares me."

"The Bible says that the two will become one flesh. Marriage is all about two wholes becoming one. I am your rib. You wanted a female version of you, well you got it. Now deal wit it." I closed my eyes and got comfortable against his chest. I didn't know if I felt one hundred percent secure in the fact that he'd not done anything inside of that room with Jazzy, especially because of how she was dressed, and was always dressed, but I was forced to let the moment pass until a later date. Had I not been pregnant, I would have been all over her ass like spots on a leopard.

T.J. & Jelissa

Chapter 12
Bentley

"Yo, I told you it was sweet as hell. While everybody else is going through the front door and getting patted down, before they walk through the metal detector, Jazzy let us in through the back, and all is well. How much sweeter can it get?" Lethal said, cocking one of the two Forty Fives that he carried on his hip. He screwed in a silencer into one and then the other, with a grin on his face.

We were in Tallahassee, in the bathroom of the banquet hall that the bachelor party was set to take place in. While the other partygoers were entering into the front of the hall, me and Lethal had been let in through the back of it by Jazzy, who in about twenty minutes was preparing to jump out of a cake that the best man had kept in the main kitchen.

I screwed the silencer into my nine millimeter. "Yeah, so far so good. Let's just hope the rest of the mission go just as smooth," I said, looking him over from the corners of my eyes. I didn't trust this nigga as far as I could throw him. Ever since Jazzy had put me up on game about some if the things that he'd neglected too I had come to the conclusion that Lethal was a shiesty nigga, and all out for himself. He was a drunk and a user. I couldn't trust neither of those characteristics in a man. I didn't even feel comfortable with him on this mission. But the fifty gees was needed, and I was banking on Jazzy doing her thing even more so than him.

He put his pistols into the small of his back, and flipped his shirt, then suit jacket over it. I did the same. "Yo, like I said before, Bentley, I'm supposed to hit you wit fifty bands. But as long as we handle our bidness and get out if here in a timely fashion, safe and sound, cuz, I'ma throw you an extra ten. You got my word on that. Sound like a plan?"

"Most definitely. Now, let's go and make it happen."
I looked in the mirror to make sure the handles of my guns
weren't poking out, confirmed they weren't and looked
over to him.

"Yo, remember we just chill around and shoot the
breeze until we get to the part where Jazzy do her lil rou-
tine. After she set the room on fire, that's when we take
out the couple niggas that we're supposed too, not a second earlier. You're familiar with their pictures that I sent
to your phone right?"

"Come on nigga, I ain't new to this shit. I live this.
Let's step in here and see what's good."

"Aiight cool." He flicked a piece of lint off of his
jacket. "Let's roll then."

I pulled open the door, and two dark-skinned dudes
with dreads stepped past us and into the bathroom. We
walked out into the reception area. I looked around. The
bachelor party was decorated with blue and yellow ban-
ners. There were pictures all around the reception of the
groom wearing his football uniform. The different ones in
high school, college, and now the NFL. There were also a
couple of him and the bride to be posted. There was a long
table with food and snacks on it, and a few caterers that
were tending to the guests. Music from Bruno Mars came
out of the four big speakers. The twelve dudes that were
present seemed to be talking in pairs. Laughing at whatever they were talking about. There was a big projector
screen in the middle of the banquet hall with a hardcore
porno playing on it. A few men were gathered around it.

"Yo, how did we get invited to this whole thing
again?" I asked Lethal, scanning the soirée.

He shrugged his shoulders. "Don't let it bother you,
it's underworld politics. Just know all of the right strings

have been pulled for us to be able to do what we need too. The niggas that we knocking off gotta go. That's word straight from Damo's mouth. I FaceTimed with the homie last night. Finally got him a cellphone up in there, when we finish this thang tonight, I'ma let you holler at him. That way y'all can get an understanding in regards to the whole Havana thing. Like I told you before, he's a good nigga. You'll find that out real soon. Come on."

I led the way, we stepped in front of the refreshments table. I picked up a cup of the Patron and took a sip out if it. Surveying the area over the rim of my cup. It seemed like every nigga there had dreads in his head, and not the fresh and neatly twisted ones either. I counted twelve dudes in all. That included the two male caterers that were serving the residents of the party. I leaned over to Lethal. "Yo, its twelve cats here altogether. Now I see the two that we're supposed to hit, but what about the other ten?" I needed to know, because there was no way that I was about to hit twelve people and only be getting paid fifty or sixty gees for the hit. That wasn't happening.

"Yo, it's all under control. You just worry about them two niggas over there." He pointed with his chin real subtle like at the groom, and his best man. They laughed in the corner of the room with drinks in their hands. They were close enough for me to make out their features. The groom's dreads fell past his waist. He was a light skinned man with gray eyes, and a real muscular physique. His best man was tall and skinny, with dark skin and brown eyes. I got to envisioning what smoking them would be like. Developed a hatred for them in my heart even though I'd never met them a day in my life. It was easier that way.

One hefty looking Haitian walked through the dining hall, and looked over to us, gave an angry stare, before going on his way he looked back at us one more time.

"Yo, you saw how kid looked at us, B?"

Lethal nodded. "Yeah, I wonder what all of that was about." He mugged the man as he disappeared into the back of the banquet hall.

"Fuck 'em Dunn. Yo, let's handle this shit and get up out of here." I tried to rubber neck and see where that big nigga had went. His eyes looked cold, and as if they were without a soul behind them. He had to be up to something. I knew a killer when I saw one.

The best man came and cleared his throat. "Attention everybody let me have your attention please. As we know, it's my nigga's farewell to freedom day, and I just wanna thank all of y'all for coming out to help to celebrate this with us. But, without further ado, I'd like for everybody to move the center of the banquet hall so that we can really get this celebration on the road. Grab one of those fold out chairs and place them in a circle for me, Donnie you make sure you sit in the very middle, I'll be right back." He headed toward the back of the banquet hall.

All of the men started to murmur amongst themselves. Walked to the right side of the room, and grabbed chairs, setting them up in the way the Best man asked them too.

"Yo, you chill up here and get in the circle wit these niggas, and I'ma follow dude so I can smoke his ass. That a be one down, nah mean?" He frowned and headed toward the back of the banquet hall looking both ways and behind himself.

I followed the route of the other men. Grabbed a metal fold out chair and set it in the circle that the other guys had formed. They were rubbing their hands together in anticipation. Most of them had bottles of Cîroc by their feet, or big blunts in their hands that were lit.

Some dude with long, nappy dreads handed me a big blunt out of a big Ziploc bag full of them that looked like a brown marker. "Dis comes straight from Port Au Prince, try it, you're going to love it." He winked at me, before handing one to every man in the circle, even the ones that were already smoking something.

The lights were powered as the two caterers came and sat in the circle. Then Cardi B's "Money" started to bang out of the speakers. I looked across the room and saw Lethal pushing a big chocolate cake on wheels across the floor. "Gentlemen, and gentlemen, prepare to be amazed. Get your bills out and won't be afraid to made it dollar storm up in this bitch. Introducing the fine, the sexy, the delectable, the chocolate goddess herself, Delight." He pushed the cake in front of the groom and stepped backward.

"Say man, where is Greg?"

"Oh, he handling something in the back. He said to go on, he got another surprise for you that's to follow this one."

The groom nodded. "Right on."

Lethal pulled up a chair and sat on the left side of me. "I handled that nigga, cuz. Brains splattered. It's all love, now watch Jazzy do her thing."

I nodded and looked forward. The groom fidgeted in his hair, almost impatient. "Come on bitch, I got my ones right here." He pulled a knot from his pocket and waved it in front of the cake as if it were a fan.

Lethal stood up. "How about we do a countdown for her fellas? Everybody repeat after me, one. Two. Three."

Jazzy popped out of the cake. She was dressed in a small black and white bikini top that was way too small for her as were most of the things she wore. Her chocolate breasts spilled over the tops of the material, and out of the sides. She stepped away from the cake clad in a matching thong. It looked like she'd purposely stuffed the cloth up into her sex lips, because they were exposed on each side of the material. She slow winded, dancing in front of the groom. Her flat stomach gleaned in the dim lights. She straddled his lap and began to twerk in a slow motion, holding his head. Her big booty popped and jiggled as she danced to the rhythm of the song coming out of the speakers.

He took ahold of her ass and squeezed it. Rubbed all over the flesh expanse of it. Every time he released her globes, they jiggled. He laughed. "Damn this bitch hot. I don't know if I'm ready to be married. Whew-we!" he quipped.

The other men hooted and hollered and got to throwing ones in the direction of the pair. Jazzy stood up and moved her body like a snake. Bent all the way over and touched her toes. Mover her ass from side to side, then slid her hand between her legs, pulling the material to the side to expose her freshly shaved, chocolate delight. It was so fat that my mouth dropped open. I couldn't stop my dick from jumping in my pants. It had been two weeks since me and Jade had done anything sexual, and my nature was calling like a bill collector. Seeing that fat pussy, and how thick them thighs were started to affect me in the wrong way. Me and Jade had to do something soon. I needed her to relieve this beast in me.

She dropped down and hit the splits. Came to all fours. Spread her knees and started to pop that ass hard with her pretty face on the floor. Then her ass was clapping, mesmerizing everybody it seemed. She looked back over her shoulder at me and licked her lips. Smiled, and got to popping so hard that her titties jiggled out of her bra. Both breasts were exposed. She cupped the first one and pulled on the nipples with her fingers.

Now my piece was hurting. It had somehow wormed it's way past my waist band and stood straight up past my navel throbbing. Jazzy flipped on to her back and opened her legs wide. Running her fingers through her pussy lips, before dipping it inside of herself and shuddering. She looked directly into my eyes, then sucked her finger.

I missed Jade. I needed to be with my baby. I had to buss this move, get the fuck home, so I could lay pipe to her the right way. I just hoped she was feeling better. I needed for her to be in a halfway sexual mood. I was begging the heavens above with my piece jerking over and over.

Jazzy slid back to all fours and stood up. Gingerly walked to the cake that she stepped out of and bent over, moving her juicy booty from right to left, then from left to right, reaching inside of the cake.

The groom stood up and smacked her on the ass. "Hell yeah! I gotta fuck this bitch! This gon be the last piece of pussy I get before I become a married man. My fiancée just gon have to—"

Jazzy turned around with two guns in her hand and began firing on him. Six quick shots sent him flying backward with massive holes in his face. Then her gun was turned on the rest of the men in the circle with the exception of me and Lethal. She fired rapid and hit her targets over and over as they began to scatter all over the banquet hall.

"Hell yeah! Pop that bitch, baby. Pop that shit!"

Men continued to fall. Some struggled to get back to their feet. I scooted my chair all the way back, and stood up, whenever I saw one that she'd missed or appeared to be getting away. The nine caught 'em slipping and sent them on their way. Before it was all said and done we stood while the twelve men in the circle lay lifeless. Our guns smoking like a barbecue grill.

Lethal jumped up excitedly. "Now that's how you do that shit. That's how you come in this bitch and ice twelve muthafuckas and fulfill a contract. That's why I love you, Jazzy." He made his way over to her.

Boom. Boom. Boom. Boom.

Big holes filled Lethal's back. He fell forward into Jazzy's arms. They crumbled to the floor with him shaking like crazy.

I flipped backward in my chair and spotted the big Haitian from earlier. He turned to run toward the back of the banquet hall. I aimed and fired. *Whoof. Whoof. Whoof. Whoof.* The silenced nine spit over and over. Each one whizzed past him and slammed into the wall directly in front of him knocking big chunks out of the brick wall. He fell to the floor on one knee, bussing in my direction back to back. His slugs crashed into the big projector that the smut movie was playing on. The screen exploded and began to smoke, before fire erupted from it. He sent three more shots and turned to run down the long corridor that led to the veranda and the exit.

Jazzy took off running behind him. *Boom. Boom. Boom. Boom.* The gun jumped in her hand. The shells leaped from it, she kept on running toward him. Stopped after a few strides to try and shoot again, but the gun jammed. Out of anger she threw it in the direction of him. "Muthafucka! Argh!" she screamed.

He threw his back against the wall of the hallway and sent two more shots her way. She screamed and been to run away. This made him chase her squeezing his pistol over and over. He must of been a real bad shot, because while his bullets smacked into a bunch of stuff in front of her, none of them managed to hit him, and by all of the attention being on her, he stupidly forgot about me until it was too late.

I stood, aimed and fired, pulling the trigger over and over again. He flew backward into one of the long tables and fell over it. His gun slid across the floor. I broke into a sprint, stopped, and stood over him for a second. He made a mock attempt to crawl toward his gun. Groaning and moaning. He left a trail of blood along the way.

Jazzy came and picked up his gun. Balled up her face, then slammed her bare foot into his back, knocking him to the floor. "Turn over, Seth! Now!" she ordered.

He groaned. "Fuck you, bitch. Fuck you!" He rolled on to his side. His shirt became matted to his chest, drenched in blood, but he refused to turn over.

I grabbed his arm and flipped him on to his back and stood back. "Hurry up and smoke his Bitch ass. We gotta get out of here." I said looking around. There were bodies in every direction that I looked. Seemed like I was in a bad war movie or something.

"Yousa pussy Seth. You betrayed my brother. He did everything for you, and you still went over to his enemies. I hate you!" she screamed.

"Fuck Damo! That nigga don't care about nobody but his self. I don't owe no loyalty to him. He gon fuck you over to. He's a..."

Boom. Boom. Boom. Boom. She sent four shots into his face, causing it to leap from the ground over and over. Then she was standing over him with her gun smoking. "Seth ain't nothin but a turn coat. My brother helped his bitch ass buy his first house and this is the thanks he gets? He tries to kill his little sister?" She kicked him in the ribs with her barefoot.

I glanced over to Lethal. He struggled to pull himself on to a chair, but only wound up knocking it over. He fell on his back and lay there breathing scratchy and real heavy.

Jazzy followed me over to him. I looked down on him and shook my head. I ain't feel nothing. Since we'd been jamming he'd done nothing but told me one lie after the next. I was secretly looking for the right time to break away from him all along. But I was hoping that it would have been after me and Jade sailed away from the United States.

Jazzy knelt on the side of him. "Damn, Lethal. This is fucked up."

He opened his mouth wide, tried to say a word but nothing but blood came out. His eyes were bucked, and his arms were shaking. Two big holes appeared to be in his chest.

"What you gon do. This nigga is on his way out. Look at him. He struggling right now." I said taking a step back. There was a puddle of blood forming around his body.

Jazzy kissed him on the cheek and stood up. "Bye, Lethal." Boom.

"So what does this mean?"

"What are you talking about?" she asked.

"You know what I needed this nigga to make happen for me. But he gone now. So what does that mean?"

"Bentley, you just saved my life. If you hadn't popped Seth when you did, he would have killed me. I'm in your debt. I'ma help you get out of this country. You and Jade. My brother was the one pulling the strings for y'all anyway, instead of using Lethal, its time you go straight to the source. He'll help you get your money all the way up, before you set sail, and so will I. I knew there was a reason that I liked you so hard." She stood on tippy toes and kissed my cheek. "I gotchu, Bentley, trust me when I tell you that."

T.J. & Jelissa

Chapter 13
Jade

I closed my eyes as one of the Asian ladies sat beside me taking her time to perfect my French manicure. Below, her coworker sat on a small stool with my feet propped up so she could take the time to give me a nice calf massage, before she was to give me a matching pedicure. The massage felt so good that it made me drowsy.

Whenever I was stressed out and depressed, or my mind would not stop racing me being pampered was the one thing that I could look forward to easing my heart and mind. We had officially been in Miami for five whole months, and I was more stressed out now than I had ever been ever since Bentley and I had chosen to collectively embark on this journey. My stomach was poked out and looked like I was getting ready to blow at any second. I was starting to worry more and more about the birthing process. I worried that I would not be able to handle the pain. I had reoccurring dreams of the authorities striking at the same time I was set to have our baby and forcing me to give birth while shackles decorated my wrist and ankles. I wondered what the next step would be once our child came. We were on the run. Even though we didn't appear in the *World News* as much as we had before, there were still tikes when they'd out up our pictures and give the back story for us. That increased my anxiety.

Then when it came to Bentley, to me it felt as if he was changing. Our sex life had dwindled to barely any at all, and I felt that because of this that Bentley took to trapping harder in the streets. He came home at odds hours of the night, only to drop off large sums of cash. He'd climb into the bed briefly, kiss my forehead, and pull up my shirt so he could talk to my stomach. Then he'd plant what seemed like a million kisses all over it. And back to the streets for him. Our connection had become faint. He seemed to be inside of his own world, and me inside of my own lately. I worried about our long term relationship. I still loved my man, but the stress of our situation was getting the better of the both of us. I wondered if we'd ever be able to leave the United States behind?

The other Asian woman pulled my right foot out of the cleansing foot massager and dried it. Minutes later, she was working on my pedicure, speaking in a foreign language to the woman that worked on my hands. They laughed about something and kept right in working. There was an ethnic song that played out of the shop's speakers. It was soothing, and different. I kept my eyes closed, and exhaled. I wanted my mind to drift away to a faraway place where things weren't as complicated as they were. A mystical land where me and Bentley were still madly in love with one another, and we didn't have an army of people looking for us to bring us to our demise. The thought allowed for me to force a smile.

The door to the shop opened and closed. "Oh my God, you gotta be kidding me. Jade!" came a female's voice.

My eyes popped open out of sheer terror. Who could possibly be calling my name? I was in Miami. Stayed to myself and was hundreds and hundreds of miles away from New York. I looked toward the front door and almost crapped in my pants at the sight of Josie, my mother's youngest sister. "Josie?"

"That is you, girl!" She rushed over to my chair and started to hug me like she hadn't seen me in fifty years. "And you pregnant? Oh my God, baby. Since when?" She hugged me tighter and stood back to look me over.

My aunt Josie and my mother were really close. Whenever my mother had the nerve to vent her problems to anyone outside of me, she usually chose to FaceTime with my aunt. Out of all of our relatives on my mother's side, my aunt Josie was the one that felt most like family too me.

She was five feet three inches tall, caramel-skinned, with brown eyes, thirty and had a gorgeous figure. She had light freckles on her face as well. From ages eighteen to twenty-seven, she'd been a stripper.

The Asian women looked annoyed. The one that was doing my toes stood up and crossed her arms. "Hey, dis bitness. You hug and be lesbian later. We work now. Okay?" She rolled her eyes and sat back on her stool.

Josie stepped back and slammed her hand on her hip. "Bitch, excuse me? You better get yo life."

"Auntie, what are you doing here in Miami?"

"Girl, I own two clubs down here and got my lil real estate thing going. Yo auntie done came a long way. What are you doing down here? Please tell me that what they're saying on the news ain't true. Not my niece. I will never believe it. You were always a little angel." She covered her mouth with her hand.

"It's not, and shssh." I mugged her. Looked from one Asian lady unto the next. "We'll talk about this after they finish my treatment. You came in here for one too, right?"

She nodded. "Girl, yeah, but, now that I've seen you, I don't know what to do. I feel like breaking down in tears."

"Well don't. Let's get these treatments, and we'll talk later over lunch. How does that sound?"

She touched my arm and smiled. "It sounds great, baby. I'm just glad that you're okay." She kissed my cheek, then sat in the chair that was two over from mine, as a pair of Asian women stepped over to her to do her manicure and pedicure.

To say that I wasn't worried and completely caught off guard would have been an understatement. The last time I'd seen my aunt, I'd been sixteen years old, and her and my mother had been arguing like crazy in the hallway of the Red Hook Houses, for what I didn't know. I had to think things over clearly before I got into a long conversation with her. Her knowing that I resided in Miami was extremely dangerous to the safety and wellbeing of me and Bentley.

***

Two hours later, we were seated inside of the Olive Garden. I sat across from Josie as she forked up a nice amount of her chicken salad and placed it inside her mouth. It was covered with cheese and ranch dressing. She chewed the entire mouthful and pointed at me with her fork. We'd been talking about the night my mother had killed my father.

"Girl." She smacked. "I knew your father was crazy from the very beginning and I told you mother to not give him the time of day, but she did it anyway and he been kicking her ass ever since their wedding night, did you know that?" she asked, grabbing her diet Pepsi, sucking it threw the straw.

I shook my head. "No, I didn't. Why would he beat her on such a special day?"

"Because she came down on her cycle. Now ain't that something? That should have told her right there he was crazy. I knew she was gon have to kill him in order to break away. I can't for the life of me understand why she'd blame such a heinous act on you, but I guess a person reveals their true colors when their back is against the wall.

What a shame. They said you did a bunch of other stuff too, how true is all of that? You really help kill a policeman?"

I scanned the crowded restaurant. It was filled with a bunch of white families enjoying their Sunday lunches. They must've came right from church is what I surmised. "Josie, keep your voice down. Jesus Christ. You act like you're talking about something normal," I whispered, chastising her.

She looked around. "Girl, my fault. You know I ain't got no damn filter."

"Well, you need to get one. This is my life we're talking about here. Damn." She was getting me vexed.

"Well, excuse me."

"But to answer your question, no, I didn't help in killing no cop. That man was beating me senseless. He was on the way to killing me when my man got him the hell off of me the best way he knew how. The media is blowing that out of proportion. Trust me on that."

"A million dollars, Jade. They are offering a million dollars for your capture. That is life-changing money. I can't understand how you've been free for this long. You have to thank God for that." She forked up more of her salad. "Where is your man now? He still around?"

I shot daggers at her. "You're asking a whole lot of questions, Josie. You got a reason for asking so many got damn questions?" I snapped.

She bucked her eyes. "Chill out, baby. I got somebody you gon wanna talk to. Wait." She sucked her fingers and pulled out her phone. Typed away on the keypad and smiled. "You can thank me later." Took a sip of her soda pop. "Hello, wait a minute. Huh." She handed the phone across the table.

I pushed her hand away. "Un-un. Who the hell is that?"

"Girl, let me just put it on speaker phone." She did. "Hello, baby, are you there?"

"Yes, Auntie, I'm here. What are you doing?"

Tears dripped from my eyes. I knew my little sister, Ashland's, voice from anywhere. "Ashland, is that you, little sister?"

"Yes, who is that?"

I squeezed my eyelids tight. More tears slid down my cheeks. I envisioned the face of my baby sister the last time I'd been blessed to see her or her twin Ashley. They had been locked in a room crying. Our parents were somewhere in the front of the house, trying to kill one another. This night, my father would ultimately come out on the losing end of that bout. He would not only lose the fight, but his life as well.

"Hello? Who is this?"

I wiped the tears from my face. "It's me, Ashland. It's Jade, and I miss you so, so much. How have you been?"

There was a moment of silence as if it was taking some time for it to sink in as to whom she was talking too. "Wait a minute, my big sister Jade. Is this her?" She sounded optimistic.

"Yes. Ashland, where is Ashley, and how are you doing?"

"Ashley! Ashley! Hurry up, it's our big sissy Jade on the phone. She's alive!" she hollered.

More tears fell from my eyes. I felt so emotional that I couldn't stop shaking. I was on the verge of losing myself right there in that restaurant. I was so close to not caring about holding it together. I felt like I'd been holding it together for so, so long. Didn't know how much strength I had left.

"Jade, is that you?" came Ashley's voice.

"Yes sissy, it's me, and I love you so much."

"Jade, are you coming to live at our new house with Aunt Josie?" Ashland asked.

I looked over to Josie, who was smiling amusingly, sipping soda pop through her straw. She batted her eyelashes in a flirtatious manner, trying to be funny. "Auntie, they stay with you?"

She nodded. "They sure do. Your mother gave me temporary custody of them. The courts granted it three months ago."

"Where is my mother?" I wanted to know.

"She is where she needs to be, in a mental institution trying to get her mind right. The last time I visited her and these little girls they were getting out of foster care, and she was as drunk as a skunk with a bottle of Jack Daniels. Cursing and talking to herself. It was sad, baby. Trust me when I tell you that."

"Jade, did you leave again?" Ashland whined.

"Please don't go again, Jade, we love you," Ashley added.

"No, I'm here, babies. I'm still here, and I'm not leaving you two again. I was just talking to Auntie."

"Do you wanna see them, Jade? Huh? Your sisters are right here in Miami, and if you want to, I'll take you to see them."

I lowered my head, nodding furiously. "Yes. Yes, I miss them so much. I gotta see them. Before I lose my mind, I have to see my sisters."

***

I cannot fully describe what I felt when both Ashley, and Ashland ran into my arms and wrapped their little ones around me, crying tears of sadness and joy two hours later at Josie's town home just off of Miami Beach. As soon as she opened the door to her place, I stepped inside. The kids had been laying on their stomachs inside her living room playing on their tablets, while a nanny folded clothes and listened to Spanish music in the dining room.

"Girls, your sister is here!" Josie yelled.

They looked toward her voice, saw me and jumped up at the same time, before rushing me at full speed. The next thing I knew, we were on the floor of the front room hugging and crying, talking about how much we'd missed each other.

Later this night, we sat around a box of pizza and did the best we could to catch up. I couldn't believe how grown they'd gotten in just over a seven-month period. Their faces were leaner. They'd grown a few inches, and spoke more eloquently than I remembered, and it blew my mind because they were only a few months past their sixth birthdays.

Josie tapped away at her laptop in the other room and talked on her cellphone loudly. She appeared to be giving orders to somebody in regards to one of her strip clubs. Whenever she hung up the phone, she would go back to typing on her computer.

"Jade, are you going to have a baby soon?" Ashley asked.

"Yeah, and are you going to take us away with you? We wanna live with you, Jade. Mama don't want us no more and we're scared of her. Look, Jade," Ashland said, turning around.

Ashley raised up her shirt, and the sight of Ashland's back broke me to my knees. "I got some new ones too and they burn, Jade. They burn every time I get in the shower," Ashley said, with her voice quivering.

I covered my face with my hands sobbing into them. Looked up to my little sister's back and saw what had to be at least fifty cigarette burns all over it. I knew they had been inflicted by a cigarette, because her scars were identical to the ones that decorated my back.

Ashland pulled up Ashley's shirt to show me her new ones as well. Ashley's looked identical to hers. The wounds were covered by scar tissue. I couldn't believe the sight of it. It appeared my mother was back up to her old tricks.

"Did Mama do this?"

Both girls nodded at the same time.

I pulled them into my embrace and put my arms around them. "I love you guys, and I'm not going to allow for you to be hurt anymore. I swear on my life. I'll die before I allow for either of you to reach harm again."

T.J. & Jelissa

Chapter 14
Bentley

Jazzy sat on the couch inside of the Best Western Hotel suite and opened her Prada bag. Stuck her hand inside of it and started to pull out one stack of money after the next. She lined them along the glass table, looked up to me and smiled. "When I told you we was gon get right wit this one, was I lying?" She continued to load the table with cash.

I unsnapped my Kevlar vest, and dropped it to the floor. Picked up the bottle of Patron and popped the cork, taking a sip out of it. "That should be two hundred gees right? That mean a hunnit a piece. Am I right?"

She nodded. "A hunnit a piece. Just like clockwork. I told you I had you. Let Lethal rest in peace." She laughed.

I sat on the couch across from her and set both of my pistols on the table. We'd just gotten back from pulling a move where I watched Jazzy smoke two females at a strip club before giving me the go ahead to rape the safe in the manager's office. The lick had been casted upon me in the last minute, but at the mentioning of two hundred thousand dollars, it was one that I couldn't pass up. I didn't even have to buss my gun. She bussed hers and all I'd done was watched her back. Now I was sure to be a hundred thousand dollars richer. This would push my paper up to five hundred thousand all together. Me and Jade had more than enough to venture off into our new life. I took another swallow from the liquor. It bribed the back of my throat. The after taste rose through my nostrils.

She laid all of the money out and counted it by tens. "Yo, this two hundred and fifty thousand, kid. You and I vet a hundred thousand a piece and I'ma hit my brother with the side fifty for putting us up on the lick. He can use it to make way with his case. It's looking like he'll be coming from under that in less than three months. He's down to one murder, and it's looking real shaky, since all of the witnesses keep on coming up short." She winked at me and started tossing stacks of money into the Prada bag, before throwing the bag over to me. "I say we celebrate." She bounced up and picked up the phone.

I got to going through the bag and counting my money stack by stack until it totaled a hundred gees. Only then did I close and set the bag on the side of my foot. "Yo, when we riding back to Miami?" I asked, missing Jade. I hadn't seen her in a day and a half. Had been in the streets grinding, trying to find and hit as many licks as possible. Needed to get me and Jade as close to the one million-dollar mark as possible before we set sail. I didn't want for her or our child to need for anything. I didn't care about myself. They were my priority.

Jazzy hung up the phone after placing a bunch of or-ders. "Damn, Bentley. I just put a hundred thousand dol-lars in your pocket. You ain't have to do shit and you ready to leave me already? Some gratitude you got." She walked up to me and hugged my waist. Laid her head on my chest. "I just wanna spend a little time with you before you go. Is that so bad?"

I held her for a minute, until I started to feel some type of way. Once Jade popped into my mind, and the thought of our unborn child, I eased out of her embrace. "Nah shorty, that ain't so bad, but you already know we agreed to keep this shit professional. I got a whole ass wife, with a baby on the way. I'm tryna do right by her. She deserve that."

Jazzy frowned and turned it into a quick smile. "You're right, Bentley. I know that y'all been through a lot, and you're such a good man. That's one thing I can't take from you." She took off her Prada spring jacket and dropped it in on the short couch. Under it she wore a black wife beater that conformed to her breasts. They spilled out the sides. "We gon roll back to Miami the first thing in the morning. I'm too tired to be driving right now, plus these Fort Lauderdale police are racist ass holes. If they catch us on the road up here, they'll take us to the station and book us in, run our information until they find out who we are. It's happened to me and Lethal more than once. The last time they extradited him all the way back to New Jersey."

I thought about that for a second. That was the last thing I needed. Me or Jade. We finally had a nice amount of money set aside, now all we had to do was set sail. I couldn't risk driving on the roads and being pulled over. That wasn't an option.

Jazzy unbuttoned her tight black pants, sat on the bed and pulled them down her thick thighs. Underneath was a pair of red laced panties. She threw the pants to the side. "We can chill together, Bentley. I ain't gon bite you. I'll be a good vampire." She ran her tongue over her upper row of teeth.

I had to laugh at that. "Yo, you wiling, shorty." I shook my head and plopped on the couch. "You order somethin' to eat for us?"

She smiled. "I like how you said that?"

"Said what?" I grabbed the menu off of the table and started to look it over.

"For us. It just sounded so good." She walked over and sat across from me, sucking on her thumb. "I ordered us a couple steaks, well done, baked potato, macaroni and cheese, and champagne."

"The food sound good. I ain't no big champagne fan, but we'll make do." I grabbed the remote and flipped over to

Sports Center. I wanted to see what LeBron had done the night before.

There was a knock at the door. "Well, you need to put something in your stomach anyway. We ain't ate nothin' all day long." She got up to answer the door. Her panties were all up in her ass. Both cheeks were bare and jiggling with each step she took, along with her thighs. Just the sight of all of that, and not having been physically intimate with Jade in a few days caused my manhood to rise and harden. It didn't help that I'd peeped how perfect her toes were. There something about a woman's toes when they were kept up that did something to me, especially when the rest of their body was up to par like hers was. I adjusted my dick and stood up. Went into the bathroom and ran cold water on my wrists to settle my piece down. I couldn't have been in there more than five minutes. When I came out, Jazzy was standing in front of the door tonguing down a thick ass caramel female that wore a black Fendi trench coat. Jazzy had her up against the door with her hands all over her body. My dick shot right back up again. Throbbing like crazy. Jazzy broke the kiss and looked back at me. "The food on the table, Bentley, eat until you get full because that's what I'm about to make this bitch do. Drop that coat baby, show my mans what you working wit, I can already see how hard his dick is." She looked into my eyes and made me feel some type of way.

The caramel chick dropped her coat, and exposed her rounded ass, and hefty thighs. Her body looked silky smooth, and shiny. I could smell her perfume from where I stood, and its aroma was intoxicating. I needed to get out of there. My defenses were getting weaker. Especially when she popped back on her legs and made her thing disappear inside other ass cheeks.

Jazzy gripped her backside, rubbed all over it, all the while looking into my eyes. "We about to have some fun, Bentley. You sure you don't wanna join us? If you're having a problem with your conscience, just pop a few of these pills, and they'll ease you." She grabbed a jar of them from the nightstand.

"I'm good, shorty. Y'all gon 'head and do your thing. I'm finna feed my face." I looked down and over the food on the table.

"You sure you can eat with that big ol dick jumping in your pants like that?" Jazzy pointed.

I sat on the couch with it throbbing like crazy. My stomach growled. I grabbed the utensils and set one of the steaks in front of me. Cut a nice piece and popped it into my mouth.

Jazzy slowly stripped the caramel chick. Took her bra off and threw it next to the couch. Next came the woman's panties. She pulled them down her thighs. The strip of the thing appeared to be lodged too deep before it came out of her ass crack and slid down her thighs. She bent all the way over. The folds between her thighs exposed themselves, before she spread her knees apart. Jazzy shuddered, looking between them. "Damn, she right, Bentley. Are you getting all of this?" She licked her lips and trailed her forefinger up and down in between the woman's dark gates.

I was trying my best to not look over there, but I just couldn't take my eyes away from the scene playing out before me on the bed. My piece was jumping up and down like a NBA player.

Jazzy crawled backward off of the bed and pulled her tank top all the way off. Then slid her panties down her thighs and off her pretty toes. She crawled back on the bed and in between the caramel woman's legs where they got to tonguing each other down all loud and shit. I could hear their spit being exchanged as their lips sucked on each other's. The scents of their perfumes traveled over to me. I closed my eyes and tried to imagine Jade, and how she'd looked the last time I'd seen her naked. She'd been walking from the bedroom into the bathroom with her lil pregnant belly all poked out. A towel draped over her shoulders, when I slid behind her to kiss on her neck she'd pushed me away and said not right now, that she had a headache. I remembered feeling so rejected, and just a bit frustrated. Before she returned, I was back in the streets trying to sniff out a bag of cash.

Jazzy laid back on the pillow, while the caramel chick opened her chocolate thighs wide, and licked up and down her pussy lips. She spread them, exposing her inner pink, and slowly slid a finger deep into her hole. Pulled it out and sucked her just juices off of them. "Mmm."

Jazzy's tongue traced her own lips. She sucked on the bottom one and glanced over to me squeezing her titties together. The nipples stood up from her mounds. She pulled on them. "I want you, Bentley. I swear to God, I want you so bad, daddy. Un, damn, bitch. Yes. Eat this pussy. Un. Bentley. You see this shit, daddy? Fuck." She forced the chick's head further into her gap and threw her ankles over her shoulder blades. She frowned her face and opened her mouth wide moaning like crazy.

Whatever the caramel sista was doing between her legs it sounded wet. She slurped and groaned as she ate that pussy like a champion. Forcing Jazzy's knees to her chest, while she herself was on all fours with her pussy bussed wide open for my view. Cream oozed out of her cat and dropped down her right inner thigh. It looked so good.

I was on the couch struggling. My hand was inside of my pants. My fists pumped my piece up and down, before squeezing it hard. I was so horny that I didn't know what to do. Then the earthly stench of pussy was heavy in the air. It smelled like heaven.

"Uh. Uh. I'm cumming. Oh shit. Bentley, she got me cumming! Aw. Aw. Aw!"

The caramel chick made her cum then sucked all over her thighs. Licked along her waist and took two fingers and moved them from side to side real fast in Jazzy's pussy. Sucking the fingers into her mouth off and on. Then she was back in between her legs.

Jazzy got up and bent over. Held the headboard and laid her face on it. "Eat me from the back, bitch. Eat this pussy from the back." She reached under her belly and held her lips wide open. By the way the bed was centered, and the couch was situated I could see her pussy as clear as day. The dark lips, and the pink inwards that looked like bubble gum. I was going through it.

The caramel chick knelt behind her and stuck her face in her gap eating away. Munching, and slurping. Fingering, and rubbing all over her thick ass.

"Uhh, Bentley. Uhh, daddy. You gotta. Uh. Shit. You gotta give me some. Fuck. Of that dick. Uh. Please?" She closed her eyes and stuck her ass back into ol girl's face and came hard.

I turned the bottle of Patrón all the way up and downed half of it. Struggling. My body was driving me insane as I watched. Suddenly I got hot. Felt tingles going all through me and I couldn't take it no more. My dick was out. I pumped it looking over the scene. My eighteen-year-old hormones were working against my better judgement. I saw the caramel chick playing with Jazzy's clit. She pinched it, then sucked it into her mouth, fingered her hard and fast.

Jazzy shook. Clenched her teeth together. Her eyes had been closed, so when she opened them and saw that my piece was out and that I sat there on the couch stroking it, she rolled on to her side and nudged the caramel chick away from her. The next thing I knew, she was on the side of me with my dick in her hand stroking it.

"Mmm, Bentley. Damn this a big dick, baby. You gotta let me sit on this. You just got to. I just made you a hunnit thousand dollars, daddy. Even a pimp's bitch would have earned his dick for the night in that case." She kissed the head and licked all around it.

I downed more of the Patrón. My head felt cloudy. My eyes were low. The feeling of her warm hand on my pipe felt so good. She squeezed it and moved it up and down. Her mouth trapped the head and sucked hard. I could feel her tongue twirling around and around it. Fuck, I done let this bitch put my dick her mouth. The lines had been crossed. I felt guilty. Bogus. I would never forgive myself. My head got to spinning. I wanted to push her away but couldn't find the strength nor the determination to do so. I was screwed.

Jazzy licked along the length of me, then angled my dick so she could suck it at full speed, pumping it at the same time, causing my eyes to roll into the back of my head.

The caramel chick sat eagle on the table in front of us and fingered her pussy with lightning speed, while she cupped her left breast. Her hard nipple crept through the crack of her finger. She pinched it and moaned out loud. "Jazzy? Un! Baby. Who is he to you? Tell me? He so fine." Her fingers dipped in and out of her box. Every time she pulled them out they were wetter than before. There was a puddle forming under her ass cheeks.

Jazzy began to work me over. She sucked me with blazing speed gagging every few seconds. Then she popped my dick out and lick all around the head, nipping at it with her teeth ever so slightly, causing me to shudder. "Dis gon be my daddy right here. I'm gon turn his ass out. Watch me." she bragged, pumping my piece, before sucking it back into her mouth and really going into overdrive.

I felt numb. My whole body felt like it was buzzing. I could feel her wetness swallowing and slurping on me, but nothing more. I tried to get up to push her away, but I was stuck. Felt like a ton of bricks was on my chest.

The caramel chick got off of the table and crawled across the floor on her hands and knees. Knelt beside Jazzy and started to rub all over her. "Let me taste him too, Jazzy. Let me suck that mafucka. Please."

Jazzy increased her speeds looking up at me, then with a loud popping sound, dislodged me from her mouth, and leaned it over to the caramel chick.

"Nall shorty, don't," I mustered, and once again tried to get up from my seated position. But I couldn't.

The caramel chick slid me into her mouth, and I got to shaking because everything became so sensitive and hyper-sexual. As soon as I entered her mouth, I came. "Mmm. Mmm. Mmm." She moaned and kept on sucking me. Rubbed all over my abs and stood up when she had my dick even harder than it was before. Rubbed her bald pussy. "Let me ride this nigga, Jazzy." She tried to straddle my lap.

Jazzy pulled her off. "Hell n'all. He finna be my nigga. If anybody gon ride his dick, it's gon be me." She opened her juicy lips, and straddled my lap, bumping her kitty into the stalk of my pole.

"Well, I'm next then." The caramel chick sat beside me on the couch and kissed my neck. That Mollie and them Percocets got yo ass numb don't they, daddy? I know, it's the best quality in all of Florida. All you gotta do is fall back and let is handle our bidness." She rubbed my chest and started to kiss me some more, turning my head so she could get my lips.

"Mollie and Percocets? What the fuck she talking 'bout? I ain't popped shit" I said, feeling like I was running out of breath.

Jazzy licked my neck. "You good, daddy. Just let me take care of you." She grabbed my dick, and slowly eased down onto it. Her eyes were bucked. I could feel my pole sliding into her scorching cave, until she'd fully inhaled my tool. She took ahold of my shoulders. "Huh. Huh. Huh. Okay. Awright, let's watch the baby ride this dick better than Jade or Keri ever did." The next thing I knew, she was bouncing up and down in my lap, moaning at the top of her lungs. No matter how hard I tried to gather the strength to push her off of me, I could not. I was too weak, and my body was screaming for sexual release. So she rode and rode me until she passed out on top of me screaming that I was her daddy. By the time she finished, the caramel chick had left.

Chapter 15
Jade

I could hear Bentley's key sliding into the lock. Then the sound of him dropping it. "Ashland, Ashley come here." I called to them and placed my arms around their shoulders. It was eight o' clock in the morning, two weeks after I'd rediscovered my sisters were living here in Miami. I hadn't had the chance to speak with Bentley about them. I could tell that something was wrong with him because for the last two weeks he'd been unable to look me in the eyes. I could only imagine what that meant, I wanted to ask him what the matter was, but I was too afraid of what he'd reveal. He'd been spending a lot of time with Jazzy under the guise of trapping. Time spent away from me and his home. Something within their relationship caused my soul to become uneasy. No matter how much he assured me that I could trust him, I knew deep within my heart of hearts she was still feeling him, and that given the opportunity, she would seize her moment. We'd been sexually inactive for nearly a month now. My mind had been too weighed down by the impending arrival of our child, along with the new revelation of my sisters' well-being, and the fact that I didn't know how much longer I could mentally survive being on the run. I loved my husband with everything that I was, but sex was just the last thing only mind.

Bentley finally got the door opened, and pushed it in. He stumbled inside and caught his balance. In his hand was an opened bottle of Patrón. He reeked of alcohol and weed smoke. Before he could close the door behind him, he squinted and smacked his lips at me. "You been sitting here the whole time, baby, and you couldn't open the door for me? Damn." He slammed it and left the keys on the other side. Began to walk toward our room and paused in his tracks. "Wait a minute, whose kids are these?" He pointed from one of my sisters to the other.

They hugged me tighter. I could feel the both of them shaking. They stuck their faces in between my arm pits. This pissed me off. In his drunken state, Bentley reminded me of my father. Every time he came home in one of his drunken moods, me and my sisters reacted in the same way they were acting at this time.

"These are my sisters. This one is Ashland, and this one is Ashley. You need to introduce yourself the right way. You're scaring them." I glared at him.

He wiped his mouth, and had a hard time keeping his balance. "Yo, whut up, lil shorties? How y'all doing this morning?" He closed his eyes and licked his lips.

Ashland tried to crawl all the way under my arm. "I'm scared, Jade. He smell like Daddy. He gon get us."

This freaked Ashley out as well. She tried to crawl into my other side. She was already crying tears of fear. "Is he mad at us?"

"No, babies. He's not mad at you. Tell 'em you're not mad at 'em, Bentley."

"Yo, those are kids. Why would I be mad at them?" he asked, getting irritated.

"Just tell 'em!" I snapped. "Damn. Is that so hard?"

"Man." He waved me off and made his way down the hallway. "I'm grown as hell. Fuck I look like being mad at a kid. Yo, princesses, y'all good. I don't even know y'all."

I hugged them for a moment longer, then stood up. "Look, y'all stay in here and I'll be right back, okay? I have to go in here and talk to him, as soon as I'm done I'll be right back. I promise. Until then play your tablets. Okay?"

"Are you going to fight with him like Mama did Daddy?" Ashley asked.

"Yeah, is one of you going to die?" Ashland added.

I shook my head. "No, babies. We're going to have a conversation, and that will be that. I'll be right back. Put your headphones in your ears." They followed my directives and turned on their tablets.

I turned and headed into the bedroom, when I got there Bentley was sitting on the edge of the bed with his head down. The bottle of liquor was in his right hand. In his left was his cellphone. He was on Facebook doing something.

I closed the door, and stepped in front of him, and snatched the phone out of his hand. "What the hell is your problem? Do you have any idea what those little girls have been through?" I yelled, louder than I meant to.

He didn't even bother to look up at me. "I fucked up, Jade. I made a huge mistake, and I don't know what to do." He took a long swallow from his bottle and wiped his mouth with the side of his hand. Shook his head. "Damn, I hate me."

I felt the butterflies enter into my stomach. I swallowed my spit and grew nervous. Sat on the bed beside him. "What did you do, Bentley? What has you so fucked up that you are unable to look me in my eyes?"

He hung his head. "I don't wanna talk about it. Just know that I fucked up and I'm sorry, baby. You have been the only thing that I've ever done right. I fucked up, and I wanna put a bullet in my head." He dropped the bottle of liquor and pulled a revolver from his waist. Looked over the gun, and pressed the barrel to his temple, cocking the hammer. "I don't deserve to be here. I'm a fuck nigga, Jade. On everything, I am."

I stood up and backed away from him. "What did you do, Bentley? Did you cheat on me? Oh my God. Did you cheat on me with Jazzy? That trifling bitch?" I screamed.

He shook his head. "Never baby? I would never cheat on you. You know me better than that. This is us, Jade. Until my last breath." He pressed the barrel even harder into his temple. Blinked and tears came out of his eyes. "Damn, boo."

"What did you do, Bentley? What did you do that makes you want to kill yourself? That's making you want yo leave me? Tell me now!"

"I fucked her, Jade! I don't know how and why, but we fucked!" He stood up and backed into the wall. "I would never cheat on you, baby. I don't know how that shit happened."

I felt like I'd been stabbed right through the heart with a butcher's knife. He'd cheated. With Jazzy. I should have known. "When did this happen, Bentley?"

He sunk to the floor crying. The gun now at his side. "Two weeks ago. In Fort Lauderdale. I swear to God, I didn't wanna do it, but it was like there was something else controlling me. I saw what was taking place and I couldn't stop it from happening. I'm so sorry, Jade. I love you with all of my soul, ma."

I burned a hole into the carpet with my eyes. I was so angry that I honestly had visions of killing him and Jazzy. Had my sisters not been in the living room, I probably would have, but they needed me, and I needed them. They had the only pure love on this earth for me now. Bentley had betrayed me and because of that, I could never forgive him. "You know what, Bentley, a wolf can only graze around with sheep for so long before he succumbs to the alluring effects of them. You can't change what is in your nature. I should have known that I couldn't trust you around that bitch, or around any bitch for that matter, if I'm not present. I'm not going to allow for this to ruin me.

I have to be strong for my sisters, and this baby I am carrying. As far as you and I go, we're done. You can have that bitch. Neither of you are worth my time, nor my tears. Later, nigga." I wanted so badly to break down and cry right there in front of him but the queen in me wouldn't allow for that to happen.

Before I could leave out of the room, he grabbed my wrist. "No, Jade. Baby, you can't leave me. Please. I love you way too fucking much. It wasn't my fault, baby. I swear to God, it wasn't my fault. I felt like I was drugged or some shit. You can't hold this against me. Please."

I snatched my arm away from him and pushed him as hard as I could out of my face. "Don't you fuckin' touch me ever again. We are done. All you get is one chance to fuck me over. I don't need you, or no other man for that matter. God got me." Turned the knob on the door and yanked it open. "I'll be out of here before the morning comes. I don't know where I'ma go yet, but you won't be there. I can do bad all by myself."

"What about our child, Jade? I won't let you raise our baby on your own. It's supposed to be us. I can't live without you, Jade. On my mother, I can't."

"Well, you should have thought about that before you did what you did. You didn't love me this much while you were fucking her. I bet you didn't think about me not one time, Bentley. Did you?"

"All I was thinking about was you. Baby, I couldn't fuckin' move. That bitch must have put somethin' in my drink. I'm telling you, I did not wanna do it." He grabbed me again, and pulled me to him. Held my shoulders. "Listen to me, baby. I am begging you to." His arms wrapped around me, shaking.

I shook my head. "I don't believe you, Bentley. You willingly fucked that bitch. You been wanting to fuck her since day one. I peep the way your eyes follow her around the room. Lusting, from the first day we met her inside of the Peter

McGuire Houses. You've been wanting a piece of that ever since then, and you finally got it. Well, I hope you enjoyed it. One night of passion has ruined us. It's over, Bentley. Have a nice fucking life. Now let me go."

He tightened his grip. "I ain't never letting you go. You're all I need, Jade. I swear to God you're the only person in this world that I love."

I allowed for him to hold me for a few minutes. We stood there embraced in silence. Then there was a knocking on the apartment door. "Let me go Bentley so I can answer the door." He reeked of alcohol, reminded me so much of my father that it was starting to make me sick on the stomach.

"Tell me you love me, Jade. Tell me you ain't going nowhere. I can't take you leaving me. I just can't."

I slapped at his hands. "Nigga, let me go! You lost me. You did this shit." Once again, I pushed him so hard that he fell on to the bed and bounced off of it and wound up on the floor. "Now get it through your fuckin' head. We are through. I don't need a man that's gon be a nothin, just like my father was."

Bentley remained on the ground planted on his knees with his head down. "I'm so sorry, Jade. Yo, I love you so much. I'll die without you. You gotta forgive me. Please. I can't take this shit."

I stormed out of the room, and into the living room. Jazzy was just opening the side door that connected both of the apartments. She stepped inside of ours and paused when she saw me. "Oh damn. Hey, where is Bentley? I need to holler at him for a minute." She was in a pair of tight booty shorts as usual. Her thighs all out. Her button-up shirt was unbuttoned to expose her cleavage, her breasts nearly spilling out of them.

136

"So first you fuck my husband, then you got the audacity to just walk into my house like you own this bitch? Who do you think you are?" I snapped, walking up on her.

She crossed her arms in front of her chest. "Jade, you always so full of fucking drama. Ain't nobody got time for all of that shit. Where is Bentley?"

I felt me getting ready to blow my top. "Jazzy, on everything I love, you better get the fuck out of my house asking about my man. Gone now." I bumped her ass toward the side door that was wide open.

She stumbled back a few feet and stopped, balled up her fists. "Jade, I'm trying to be real respectful of you right now because of who you are to Bentley, and because you're pregnant. But bitch, you ain't gon keep testing my patience. I throw these hands. Bitch, I'm East New York too. What's really good?"

Bentley staggered into the living room, squeezing his eyelids together, before opening them. "What's going on in here?" he asked, looking from Jazzy back to me.

"Bentley, I got the plug. My girl gon help me get y'all out of here as early as next week. We just gotta buss one move for her and its good. Are you proud of me?" She asked stepping further into the house and around me. Our shoulders brushed each other's.

I blew my top. "Proud of you? That's it." I pushed her as hard as I could back into her own apartment. Rushed inside of it and straddled her ass reigning blow after blow into her face. Her head bounced off of the carpet.

"Argh!" She flipped me off of her and straddled me. Slapped me so hard I bit my tongue. "Punk bitch! It ain't sweet." Another slap across my face that bussed my nose. Then another that split my lip.

Bentley grabbed a handful of her hair and pulled her off of me with her screaming at the top of her lungs. "She pregnant! What the fuck is wrong with you?" He picked her up and carried her about twenty paces away from me, then he set her down.

She slapped his face. "You ain't have to pull me up by my hair, you son of a bitch. Yo ho came at me bogus. I came over there to tell you that I'd did everything you told me to do like a good girl. You should be praising me right now, daddy."

"Daddy?" I rushed that bitch at blazing speed, or as fast as my pregnant belly would allow for me too. Picked her up and slung her ass into the big screen television that was hanging on the wall of her apartment. She and it fell to the floor in a big boom. I got to kicking her in the ribs, the back, and in her lil funky ass. I wished I was wearing fleets. Had I been, I would have stomped her until the entire carpet was filled with blood.

She winced in pain and balled up, covering her head with her hands. "Stop. Stop Jade. Damn."

But I kept on kicking and stomping until Bentley picked me up and carried me back into our apartment with my legs kicking wildly. I wanted him to release me. I needed to get into her ass. This bitch had been way too disrespectful. I'd had more than I could take. Seducing my man. Then fucking him. Yeah, I needed to feel my foot up her ass. It was the only way I could get over Bentley's betrayal in the moment.

"Let me go, Bentley. Let me whoop that bitch, let me whoop her ass," I screamed.

"Jade. Please take us back to Aunt Josie's. Please, Jade. We're so scared," Ashland cried.

"Baby, you're pregnant. What's the matter with you? Are you trying to lose our kid? Huh?"

"Let me down. Ashland, y'all go in the back room. Okay. Let me finish talking to my husband. Y'all don't need to see this."

Jazzy staggered into the apartment with two guns in her hands. "Move, Bentley. Move so I can kill that punk ho." She cocked the hammers on the guns. Both of them had silencers on the ends of them. If she shot, nobody would hear.

"We wanna go back wit Aunt Josie!" Ashley screamed. Y'all are crazy here!"

"Move out of my way, Bentley! This ain't got nothing to do with you! I'm tired of that bitch. You don't need her no more, all you need is me, baby. Just you and I." Jazzy grumbled. She held up both guns to try and get a clear shot at Jade.

Baby? Just her? I stared to shake from anger, trying to figure out my next move. Had I not been pregnant I would have rushed her at full speed and forced her to pull that trigger. I didn't think she had the guts to do so. Felt that she was all talk.

The twins screamed. Ran into a corner and hugged each other. Ashland shook her head. "Why? Why? Why? Please don't kill our sister. We need her," she sobbed.

Bentley remained in front of me. He was so muscular that his body was able to fully cover mine. "Yo, put that gun down, Jazzy. What the fuck is wrong with you? You scaring these lil kids."

"Fuck them lil bitches! Don't nobody care about them. Move so I can pop that broad or you gon eat these hollow points with her ass."

"Move, Bentley. I ain't scared of her. She ain't got the heart to shoot me. Do it then, Jazzy. Shoot me, bitch, or drop them guns and we can finish getting it in. Pregnancy or no pregnancy." I was ready to go.

Tears sailed down her cheeks. "Move, Bentley. I'm begging you to move, baby. I don't wanna shoot you. I don't wanna hurt you at all. We can be so good together."

Now I was vexed. I started to punch at Bentley's big back. "Move. Get the fuck out of the way. Jazzy, ain't nobody studding you. If you was 'bout that life, you would have bussed already. Either shoot or put the guns down."

"I'm sorry, Bentley. I'm sorry. Please forgive me." She aimed and lowered her eyes.

Bentley rushed her at blazing speed, grabbed both of her wrists. The guns went off and knocked holes in the ceiling. He wrapped his arms around her and carried her into her apartment.

A sharp pain went through my pelvic floor. I felt a warm liquid leaking down my inner thighs, and then another pain. This one so sharp it brought me to my knees. I felt like I couldn't breathe. Before I could overcome that, one another followed and this one forced me to fall on my side out of breath. "Bentley." I gasped. "Bentley, baby, help me. Help me."

He took both guns from Jazzy and slammed her against the wall. Spoke with his forehead against hers. I couldn't hear the words coming out of his mouth. She stood silent, staring into his eyes. He continued to chastise her, before looking over his shoulder to see me on my side in a ball.

He released her and rushed back into the house. "Holy shit, Jade!"

Another blast of pain shot through me, before I became dizzy and passed out.

Chapter 16
Bentley

I paced back and forth on the side of Jade's bed, feeling like shit. I had a hangover that had my head pounding. I'd thrown up three times, and in addition to that, I knew all of this was my fault. I should have never gotten involved with Jazzy. Had I not allowed myself to come into close confines with her, I would have never wound up being drugged, and I would have never slept with her. Jade had been right. I'd lusted over Jazzy since the first day we'd met, and secretly wondered what it would have been like to fuck her. I would have never cheated on Jade. No matter what went on get been Jazzy and myself. Lord knows that I felt lower than the sewers.

I stopped pacing and stepped over to her bed side. Placed my hand on her forehead and kept it there. Glanced over to the monitors. The constant beeping was driving me crazy. It was like with every beep, I was being constantly being reminded of all of the wrong that I'd done against my wife. Man, I felt like shit.

Jade stirred in her sleep. Jerked, and kicked her feet. Her eyes shot open. "Ashley. Ashland. Where are you?" she whispered.

I stroked her cheek with the back of my finger. "Baby, are you okay? You been out since last night, and most of today. You went into false labor. You're in a hospital right now."

She winced in pain. "A hospital? Why? Where are my sisters? Where are the twins?" She started to get up.

I forced her back down to her pillows. "Baby, chill. You're at high risk of losing our child right now or giving birth so early that there will be complications. Our child can even have birth defects. You need to fall back."

"Fall back? No. Where are my sisters? I gotta save them. Something ain't right. Where are they?"

"I left them at home. Your little sister, Ashley, gave me your aunt's number. She was coming to get them from Miami Gardens. She should have done it this morning. They're safe. You need to worry about the safety and well-being of our child. Your sisters are good."

Jade wiped her face with her hand. "Oh, okay. That's cool." She yawned and closed her eyes. Fell back on the pillow and laid there for a minute. Then her eyes shot open. "Wait a minute. You left them at home? With who?" she asked, sitting up.

I should have known she wasn't about to let his shit go. Damn, I didn't feel like arguing. The doctors were already saying she was over stressed, and that any additional stress or physical exertion could cause her to give birth two months early. And if she did so, then our child was at risk for all kinds of long-term problems. That spooked me. We were already on the run for our freedom and lives. If we gave birth to a child that needed a lot of medical attention that would make things a hundred times more difficult. I didn't know how the medical care was in Havana, but I planned on having myself and Jade in Cuba by the end of the month.

"Who did you leave them with, Bentley? Who?" Jade pulled the oxygen out of her nose, and then picked at the IVs in her left hand.

I rushed to her other side to stop her. "Baby, chill. Please. The only reason I left them with Jazzy is because I was in a rush to get you to the hospital. I didn't know what the matter with you was. I just went into action."

"You left them with her? Aw shit." She yanked the IVs out of her, then jumped out of the bed. Staggered and fell to her knees. She appeared woozy and disoriented.

I fell beside her. "Jade, what's the matter, baby? Get yo ass up and get back in the bed. Are you crazy?"

She grabbed a handful of my shirt and balled it into her fist. She squeezed her eyelids together. "Bentley, you gave our honor, our loyalty and the sanctity of our marriage to that broad. Now you've given her my sisters. If anything happens to them, I just want you to know I will never forgive you. I swore to protect them, to never allow harm to reach them ever again, and you better hope I'm able to keep that promise." She used the bed to stand up. "Now, I'm getting the hell out of here, and you're going to help me. Call that bitch to make sure she's handed my sisters off to my aunt, and I'm going to call my aunt to confirm that she did."

"Jade, you ain't going no fuckin' where. You got my baby inside of you. These people already told me you are at high-risk right now. I'd be a damn fool to let you leave this hospital." I closed, then stood in front of the door.

"Well, call yourself a damn fool, nigga, because I'm up out of here. I can't believe you left a broad that hate me with my sisters. I don't know was going on with you, or what you and that broad got going on, but ever since Lethal been out of the picture, you been making one dumb decision after the next. Now help me he out of here." She limped and threw her hospital gown around her body. Her belly protruded. She walked with her hand on her lower back, came and stood in front of me glaring.

"Baby, I don't care how crazy you looking right now. You about to lay yo ass down, until these people say you're healthy enough to leave this hospital. I understand that you're worried about those lil good girls, but you're putting them before the safety of our unborn child. I ain't about to let you do that. Now go lay down." I pointed toward the bed. "I'm finna call Jazzy on speaker phone so you can hear that your sisters are good." I pulled out my phone and scrolled down the call log. "Gon now."

Jade mugged me with absolute hatred. "Bentley. Nigga. I swear to God, if that girl has done anything to my sisters, I'ma..."

"Yeah, yeah, yeah. I heard you the first time. You can stop all that them threats and shit. Go lay down."

Bentley stop cursing at me and call yo side bitch so I can hear her tell you that my sisters are safe and sound with my aunt. Then let me use your phone so I can call to confirm that notion. I should call first. Matter fact, let me see that." She reached for the phone.

I stepped backward and clicked on Jazzy's number. The phone rang eight times before she picked up. "What it do Boo?"

I cringed. I hated when she called me all them pet names and shit. It wasn't even that type of party and she knew that. I swear I felt that she only did that type of stuff when she assumed Jade was present. I looked over to Jade and she was staring at the ceiling with her nostrils flared. I sighed. "Jazzy get off of that dumb shit. You know this ain't that."

"Jade must be listening, huh? Go figure." She paused. "What's up?"

"Yo, I know you told me that you was gon chill wit the twins until they aunt showed up to pick them up, I was just calling to make sure that happened."

"Nall, it didn't. I still got 'em." More silence.

"You what?" I asked.

144

Jade hopped out of the bed and hollered into the phone. "Why you ain't give them to my aunt?"

Jazzy exhaled into the phone. "Ho, ain't you supposed to be in labor or something? I thought one ass whoopin' was enough, you asking for a whole 'nother one, huh?" She snickered.

"Where are my sisters?"

"Bentley, you and I are going to buss this last move and it should gross us close to a million dollars. We gotta give two hundred and fifty thousand to the plug, and the rest is ours to split, only we ain't splitting it because I'ma take the cash and you gon tell the get out of jail free card for you and your drama-filled bitch. Y'all gon sail away to Havana, and I'ma go on with my life. Sound like a deal to you?"

"Where is my sisters?" Jade hollered again.

"Bitch, shut the fuck up about them punk-ass lil girls. Holy shit. You're obsessed with them. They are fine. Bentley, do we have a deal or not?"

Jade shot daggers at me. "This bitch got my sisters, Bentley. She got the twins." She fell to her knees again and broke down crying loudly.

I felt horrible. "Are they safe, Jazzy?"

She smacked her lips. "Not you too, man. Damn. Yeah, both of them are safe. I ain't that petty that I would ever fuck over them lil girls like I wanna do Jade. You better accept this deal though, because if you don't, I'ma have yo baby mama crying for the rest of her pregnancy." She broke out laughing.

That vexed me. Not only was this broad disrespecting Jade, but she'd brought some innocent children into the middle of the equation. That wasn't cool. "Yo, when do we handle this bidness? And how soon after do we get the girls back and we sail?"

"In two days. I'll be in touch, daddy. Don't hit my phone until I hit yours. Oh and tell that dumb bitch that the reason her sisters are still with me is because when I went to meet up with her aunt at Shoney's Pizza, she had the entire parking lot filled with police. I ain't going down like that, but just a heads up, they know you two are in Miami. Tick-tock, tick-tock." The call ended.

Jade climbed to her feet holding her stomach. Sat on the bed. "You finna go and get my sisters, Bentley. I don't care what you gotta do, you need to go and get my sisters, then we need to get out of here because it's only a matter of time before they close in on us." She lowered her head. "I should've been reading my Bible more. I should have been in that word. Ever since Guns got bodied, I been feeling all kinds of sinful. Demons have been all over me. Now I've brought the twins into this hell. It's not fair. You needs to go and find your side bitch and do whatever you need to do to get them back because it's not fair. They're just little girls."

"Man, I'ma do what I have too, but seriously, are they all you care about now? Are we done, Jade? That love you had for me even exist anymore?" I wanted to know. I was getting agitated. It did seem as if all she cared about were those little girls, and while I understood where she was coming from, it was beginning to make me feel some type of way.

She was quiet for a long time. "They're my sisters, Bentley. My blood. It's not even about you right now, it's all about them. It has to be. I'm sorry if you're feeling some type of ways, but that's just what it is. Get over it. This shit is your fault anyway. Don't get it twisted."

I stepped to the door. "You know what, Jade? Ever since you iced Guns, you've been acting real, real funny.

I know I fucked up by letting that bitch drug me, and even for leaving them with her. But, you have to forgive me. If you don't, there is no way we can accomplish these major tasks that are ahead of us. We need to be on the same page at all times. Right now we're divided, baby, and that's going to be damaging for us. Trust me on that."

"You know what, Bentley, I don't really trust nobody right now, especially not you. I don't know what you and Jazzy got or had going on behind my back but whatever it is, it's causing her to act in a real weird way. I can tell that this girl is in love with you. That hurts my heart dearly, but we don't have the time to dwell on how I'm feeling. We need to get my sisters back before she does something crazy to them out of her hatred of me. Please just go and do whatever you need to, or else I'm minutes away from going to get them back myself. I won't mind these pains that are shooting through my abdomen right now." She groaned and held her tummy. Fell to her knees, breathing hard, and rugged.

I ran over and pushed the nurse's button signaling for help, then knelt beside her, rubbing her back. "It's okay, baby. It's okay. I got you. I swear to God, I got you."

The nurses rushed into the room two at a time. Saw her on the floor and hurried to help her back to her feet. Got her into the bed and went to reinsert the IVs into the back of her hand.

"Go get them, baby. Please go and get my little sisters. They're all I truly have in this life," she shouted, before groaning loudly in pain.

Hearing that was like a knife straight through my heart. Now I was starting to feel all alone in the world. I felt I'd officially lost Jade now that she regained her sisters. That from here on out, it wasn't going to be about anything other than them, and their sibling relationship. I would forever be on the outside looking in. I felt so sick I was on the verge of throwing up.

A light-skinned, heavyset nurse hurried over to me and took ahold of my arm. "I'm sorry, sir, but you have to leave until we can get her situated. As soon as she's stable, we'll come down to the waiting room and contact you."

I glanced over her shoulder to Jade. They were helping her into the bed and laying her back. Two more nurses eased into the room, while the one eased me out. Then she was closing the door in my face. I stood there for a few moments peering through the window at Jade, then the blinds on her room window was closed to.

Chapter 17
Bentley

The next morning, I met up with Jazzy just outside of Miami Gardens in a little apartment complex called the Garden Apartments, right over on Alexandria Drive. The sun was just beginning to make its appearance in the sky. I felt dizzy as I smelled the aroma of the food that she cooked inside of the kitchen. She been cooking ever since I walked into the apartment. Came into the living room just to hug me and then she was right back in the kitchen throwing down. I sat on the couch fuming. I couldn't get Jade out of my mind or the thought of where our relationship might be headed. It was causing me to slip into my lowest stage of depression. I needed a drink, or maybe even a blunt.

Jazzy strolled back into the living room and set a tray that had a plate of French toast, scrambled eggs with cheese, onions and bell peppers, four sausages, a big bowl of grits, and a glass of orange juice on top of it before me. "Huh, Bentley. I want you to eat something before we go and handle this bidness tonight. I know you wiling over how yo wife shitting on you over them lil girls, but once we buss this move, you'll be able to give them back to her and y'all will be leaving the country. On to a new life. First you gotta eat something though." She sat beside me and started to cut up the French toast and sausages. Stuck the pieces on to her fork and brought it toward my lips.

I was so hungry I felt like I was about to faint. I moved my mouth. "Jazzy, why you do that shit? Why you drug me like that and force me to cheat on my woman? I thought you was more of a queen then that, shorty?"

She sighed and set the food back on the tray. "Niggas do it all the time to hoes. You wasn't tryin' to fuck wit me on that level, so I had to go for what I knew. I already told you that I been lusting over you ever since I was a teenager. Keri put that shit in my head. We used to do some real freaky stuff to each other using your image. You've been my fantasy for a long time. So, when I finally ran into you in the physical, I just couldn't contain myself. I had to have you. Plus, I done caught you jocking me a whole lot. I just feel like you were in your own way, so I had to nudge you a lil bit wit that concoction. It works every time." She scooped the food again. "Open up."

"What concoction?" I wanted to know. "What did you use to get me like that?"

She giggled. "A lil mix I like to call a for-sure thing. Mollie, Percocets, and a pinch of Visine. Put that shit in your Patrón, and that was that. It had that big ass dick even bigger than I imagined it could get. And we fucked for so long that I went from super wet, to wetter, to wet-wet, to moist, to dry. My pussy still feeling some type of way, and I hope you know that that's one of the one provisions. I gotta get some more of that dick before it's all said and done. Now open your fucking mouth so you can have you energy. Damn!"

I pushed my phone further into my pocket and curled my lip. I saw that I was going to have to smoke this bitch. She was a bit psychotic. I was forced to play my role so I could get the twins back. I opened my mouth and allowed her to slide the fork inside. Took the contents off of it and chewed, looking into her eyes.

"Shit good, ain't it?" She smiled and rubbed the side of my face. "Why it can't be us, Bentley? Why can't you and I just be together? We make such a good couple. You know I'd take care of you, don't you?" She ran her thumb over my lips, then leaned in to kiss them.

150

I jerked my head away, unable to play the role that I needed to without feeling sick to my stomach. I had already betrayed Jade in such a way by being involved with this broad. So many things had gone wrong. There was no way that I could follow through with anything intimate or sexual again.

She picked up the plate of food and threw it across the room. It crashed into the wall, and shattered. The grits spilled all over the carpet. The utensils wound up in the kitchen floor along with a few sausages. "I just don't understand, Bentley! What the fuck is so good about that bitch? Why do you love her so much? There is nothing that she's doing for you that I won't! In fact I'm the one that's bussing major moves for you. Helping you catch that bag every week, forty and fifty thousand at a time. This bitch ain't on shit. She always got her hand out for something or causing some kind of drama. She ain't uplifting you or your pockets in no way. I'm doing that. I'm that bitch! Period! So why you ain't fucking wit me? Tell me or she ain't never gon see them lil hoes again. That's on everything I love."

I wanted to go under my shirt and blow her wig back right now. This punk bitch had lost her fucking mind. I knew that she had to be a little off. I had to keep Jade's sisters in mind, regardless yo the jealousy I felt over them. I stood up. "Come mere, baby, because you're bugging right now, and you shouldn't be."

She raised her left eyebrow. "Say what?"

I laughed and saw myself blowing her fuckin' head off of her shoulders. My vision became blurry with red. The killa shit in me caused my veins to begin to throb real hard. Ye beats of my heart sped up. "I said come here, baby. You're right. Let me hold you for a minute."

She mugged me. Ran her fingers through her curly weave and licked her lips before coming into my arms. She laid her head on my chest. "Daddy, I just want you to love me. Nobody cares about me, and I want you too so bad. I just don't understand why you and I can't be together? We're so perfect for one another. Don't you see that?"

I felt ready to explode. She didn't feel right in my arms. She wasn't Jade. She was the enemy. She'd attacked my wife one too many times. She'd have to pay for her sins. There was no way around it. "Yeah baby I see it. I swear I do, but I'm just not one of them niggas. I just can't shit on the woman I was with. I'm more of a man than that. I'll stay wit you, but we gotta get Jade and her sisters out of the United States. I won't feel right as a man until I make that happen for her."

Jazzy looked up to me. "That's understandable baby. All we gotta do is hit this last lick for the million. Get our connect right, and she'll help them sail away. Then you and I can hit it in a different direction. Long as we are together we can accomplish anything, but it starts with this first move. You feel me, daddy?" She stepped on her tippy toes to kiss my lips again. She smelled like cocoa butter and perfume. I didn't know how she could be so much of a cold blooded killer on the one hand, and so smitten and soft with me on the other. She had to be Bipolar, it was the only explanation.

I closed my eyes and kissed her lips. Soft at first, then sucked on them to make thugs believable. All it took was for me to imagine her being Jade and I was able to get over the hump. She licked all over my lips. Licked them hard, and slid her hand into my pants, and my boxers so fast that it shocked me. She squeezed my pole, and ran her thumb back and forth across it, sending tingles through me.

I removed her hand and kissed her lips. Hated my dick for getting hard. But it had a mind of its own that I could

152

barely control. Turned my back to her so she couldn't see my current state. "When do we buss this move?"

"Tomorrow night, we gon handle the last few that are up against my brother. In the process we'll be able handle something for our connect and in short everybody wins. Damn, I can't wait until we get them all on a boat, then you and I can finally be together. We gon fuck up a storm. If you want me to give you a baby, I will. Our baby will be ten times more beautiful than the one Jade is carrying. You'll see. I'll eat all of the vegetables in the world if I have too."

"You ain't gotta do all that. Matter fact, don't even focus on that right now. Let's worry about this last move. Get our game plan together, and we'll go from there. You hear me?"

She walked all the way around until she was standing in front of me again. Looked into my eyes and popped back on her legs. "Daddy, do you promise me that you and I are going to be together after we ship Jade and her sisters off? The reason I ask is because I know that you really care about her. I can't really see how you'd leave her behind for me so easily."

I guess she was back to being sane. She was up and down more than the Dow Jones. "Baby, yes, you and I are going to be together. Jade has to look after her sisters. She ain't really got enough room left for me in her heart. Those little girls are her everything." I sighed and felt sick. I missed how me and Jade's relationship had been before we'd come to Miami. I didn't know if I was saying those words to Jazzy just to throw her off or if I really meant them. I think it was a little bit of both.

"Well, I ain't got nobody but me, Bentley. And if you'll have me, I'll even put you before myself. I just want to be loved by one man. No not one man, but by you. Don't let these rough edges make you forget that I am still a woman with emotional and physically connecting needs. I'm quick to buss my gun because I've been through a lot. But deep down inside of me is just a little girl yearning to be loved. Love is something I've never had." She stepped into my arms and wrapped hers around me. "If you'll love me, Bentley, I'll be the best woman you've ever had in your entire life. I got three million dollars put up of my own money. We couple that with yours and we can live a long prosperous life. I think I already love you. Ain't that nuts?"

I kept my silence and held her tight. I couldn't get Jade off of my brain. I missed her and I felt like I needed to get back right with her more than ever. My wife was slipping through my fingers. I could feel it. I couldn't let that happen. I loved her way too much. "Jazzy, let me ask you a question, and we don't have to go too far into it, but where are the twins? Can I at least see them to make sure that they're okay?"

She hugged me tighter and sighed. "Bentley, as long as you and I are good they'll be good."

***

The next night was go time. Jazzy looked across the long table at me and smiled. To the right of her was a dark-skinned female with long braids, and gray eyes. She carried on in a steady conversation with the man to the left of her. To Jazzy's left was a little girl that couldn't have been older than twelve. She picked at the fried chicken on her plate and made a disgusted look.

To my right was a heavy set dark skinned man. He was fucking his food up eating with both hands and making some of the grosses noises that I'd ever heard. Before we I'd set down at this table Jazzy had told me this man was her uncle, and the man to the left of me was her blood father. He had long dreads and a slim face. His long dreads were all white as if he'd dipped them in flour. He ate his food and smoked on a blunt at the same time. I found this odd to say the least, especially since there was a twelve-year-old girl at the table.

I didn't have an appetite to save my life. I wanted to get this mission over and done with. The sooner we took care of bidness, the sooner Made and I could be back together and sailing away from a country that looked to persecute is for crimes that we hadn't committed, and for the ones that we did commit out of pure survival. I wanted for us to make it out before she had our child. I didn't know how things would look having a newborn baby while at the same time being on the run for our lives. I was willing to do whatever it took to keep my family safe and sound. Even if my family now consisted of Jade's little sisters. I would make the proper adjustments.

Jazzy looked across the table at me and winked. Ran her tongue across her juicy lips that were painted black and had a heavy coat of lip gloss on them. She pointed with her chin at her father, and then her uncle. Lowered her eyes and frowned.

I slipped my hand under the table and felt the two pistols on my waist. Patted the handles, before attempting to pick at the food in front of me. We were set to celebrate Jazzy's uncle's sixty first birthday. According to her, he'd flown in from Haiti a day earlier so he could celebrate the event with his code family. He was her father's brother, and apparently the men were close. So close that her uncle was one of the men we were supposed to knock off in order to get the million dollars. She said that he was one of the men. She hadn't told me who the rest of the targets were. All of this shit was weird to me. But I was ready to get it over and done with. If we were set to whack her uncle then so be it. There was no sweat off of my brow.

Suddenly the lights were dimmed, and I could hear the sounds of happy birthday being sung in the distance. As the song got louder a small woman with long dread locks appeared wheeling a big cake. "Happy birthday to you. Happy birthday to you. Happy birthday to youuu." She sang, and then the whole family joined in, even Jazzy. All of the lights were cut in the house. The cake held sixty one candles whose fires cast shadows over the walls of the house.

Jazzy's uncle came to the front of the room and stood over the cake while everybody continued to sing to him. He held his weight on a cane. Smiled, and flipped his long dread locks over his shoulder. The singing died down. He held up his hand to quiet the room. "I am honored to spend this birthday with my brother's family. Before I take my throne, Simeon, I just want to let you know that I will never forget where I've come from, or what you and I have been through in order to get to where we are right now. Though my hands are now green, my heart continues to bleed for you little brother, and it always will. Jazzy, come here baby."

Through the flames of the candles I was able to see the sullen expression on Jazzy's face. She smiled and scooted back her chair. Stood up and made her way over to him while the entire room watched. When she got to the front of the room he smiled big and embraced her with a hug. Rubbed all over her back and stopped at her waist. Kissed both of her cheeks, and then her lips. He turned to address all of us. "This here is my angel. I love this girl. I don't mean any disrespect to any of you but she is my favorite. Always have been." He faced Jazzy. "Niece, as you know, I will be stepping up as king of Port Au Prince. I am rich now, with power and prestige that transcends. I want you to come to live with me. To be a part of my reign. I promise that you will never need or want for anything as long as you are under my care. You will be nothing short of a spoiled brat. That is my word to you. Simeon." He snapped his fingers.

The woman who'd brought in the cake stood up and came to the front of the room with a suitcase in her hand. She nudged the cake out of the way and set it on the table. Before walking back to her seat. The steady click clocking of her heels on the floor was the only sound before she took her seat.

Jazzy's uncle popped the suitcase and opened it. "Simeon, my brother, as a show of good faith, I have here one million dollars as a dowry for the lovely Jazzy. I promise to love, protect, strengthen, and spoil her. To keep our bloodline strong and pure."

Simeon raised his glass of champagne. "For a million dollars you can take her tonight. With that money we will be able to take our family to the next level. With you in place inside of Haiti things should be very interesting. France is now looking to do a lot of business. Long live the king," he roared.

Jazzy's uncle bowed his head and looked down at her. "Do you have anything that you'd like to say, baby girl?"

She smiled and nodded her head. "Sure." She took a deep breath. Looked over everybody in the room. "I never understood how I could be born into such a crazy family. With all of the lying, deceit, backstabbing, and sexual deviancy, it's no wonder that I am crazy as I am." She looked up to her uncle. "You're right. You have been obsessed with me since day one, or if not day one, then since my twelfth birthday." She lowered her head. "I invited my friend to this party so that it could help him to understand who I am without me having to explain it to him. This is why I'm so nuts, Bentley, it's because this is what takes place inside of the Jean family. My uncle buys me, and my father has nothing to say about it. What a life right?" She shook her head again.

"Baby, I thought everything was cool. You're making it seem as if you have a problem with this arrangement. Do you know how many women would love to be in your place? I mean after all, it's not like we're unfamiliar with each other. You're not a little girl anymore." He snickered.

Jazzy looked to him. "Finish him, Bentley." She stepped to the right of him.

I pushed my seat back and stood up. Aimed and pulled my trigger six quick times. Made sure that each one was on point to slam into this sick ass monster, and they were. One bullet filled him after the next, entered his chest and face, knocking him backward. He flew into the china cabinet behind him and shattered the glass. Big shards fell on top of his head. He touched one of the holes in his chest. Saw all of the blood and closed his eyes.

The members around the table began to scatter. Screams were emitted. Jazzy flipped the big table, pulled out her two pistols, and got to bussing at her family. "I hate you. I had you. I hate you all. Die. Die. Die," she screamed, pulling the triggers over and over again. Each spark illuminated the entire room. Over and over again. It smelled like gunpowder and burnt flesh. They moaned and groaned before the reaper took their souls away

When it was all said and done, Jazzy came and stood beside me. "They had to go, Bentley. They had to go. My family is sick. This is why I am how I am. Now that you know this will it stop you from loving me?" For the first time I actually saw tears in her eyes. She looked powerful and vulnerable at the same time with the gun in her hand.

I scanned the room. Saw all of the bodies. Smelled their stenches. My eyes trailed to the little girl. Jazzy had put so many holes in her that it was ridiculous. I felt sick to my stomach. "N'all, baby, that ain't gon stop me from moving you. Now that I know where you came from it helps me to understand who you really are. Grab that suitcase and let's go."

T.J. & Jelissa

Chapter 18
Jade

I was going crazy inside of the hotel room. All I could think about was my sisters. Bentley had been gone for two days now and had not returned any of my calls. I was worried sick and prayed that he was okay. I loved him, despite our circumstances. He'd had his phone on speaker the entire time he questioned Jazzy about the drugging of him. I now knew that the sex was not real. That she'd put something into his Patrón . She'd admitted to that fact. I'd heard her loud and clear, and the revelation had devastated me. Bentley was telling the truth the whole time. I wished I'd listened to him. I felt horrible.

I slowly eased my way out of the bed, and held my stomach. I needed to pace. My mind was getting the better of me. Since I'd not been able to give Aunt Josie any updates on my sisters she'd promise to go to the local authorities to tell them everything involving my sisters and my situation in general. The last time I'd seen the news, both me and Bentley had been plastered all over it. We were being made out to be both murders and kidnappers. There was a Florida-wide manhunt for the both of us. Time was dwindling down. If we didn't get out of Florida soon, we were toast.

The door swung open, and Bentley stepped into the room, he looked tired, and worn out. There were bags under his eyes. He closed the door and took a moment to sigh.

"Where the fuck have you been, Bentley?" I snapped, waddling over to him.

"Baby, please chill. I been out there making shit happen and it's been real crazy. Its police everywhere looking for us, we gotta go, now." He opened the closet and grabbed a duffle bag out, stuffing it with my clothes.

"Where are the twins? Where are my fucking sisters? You've been gone for two days! Two!"

He stood up. "Jade, I fucking get it. I know where I been. I been getting shit in order to make sure that we're able to sail away from this mafucka. It's real hot right now. We gotta go. Come on and get dressed."

"Why are you not telling me if my sisters are okay? Why are you avoiding answering that fucking question, Bentley?" I fell to my knees, a sharp pain shooting through my gut. I was praying that I wasn't about to go through all of that again. Because of my paranoia, I'd been forced to check out of the hospital early, despite the doctor's urging me to stay put. Lucky I did, because fifteen minutes after I broke away from there, I saw on Facebook that the entire facility was surrounded by cops.

"I ain't seen the twins yet, but Jazzy assured me that they are good, and she ain't got no reason to lie about that. I've done everything that she's asked me to. Now she gotta hold up her end of things. So, get dressed so we can meet up with her. We're setting sail today. We have to."

I felt like I was getting ready to pass out. The pain in my gut was killing me. I didn't fully understand what Bentley was talking about. The only thing I gathered was that he didn't have my sisters, and he didn't know where they were. That we were basically in Jazzy's hands. Them and us. A bitch that hated me with a passion. I was sick.

He leaned down and helped me up. "Come on, baby, just trust me on this."

I wrapped my arm around his neck. "What other choice do I have, Bentley? This bitch has got you by the balls. And because she does, she got us too. I hope you know what you're doing. I swear to God I do."

***

Jazzy's hair blew in the wind as she steered the motorboat across the water on the bright, hot, spring day. The sun was scorching. The water looked like we were boating on mouthwash. There was a heavy scent of salt in the air. "Yo, even though I don't fuck wit you, Jade, I wouldn't snuff yo sisters like that. I can't lie and say it didn't cross my mind, but I didn't. I know one thing, when you have that baby I want us to fight head-up. Win or lose, Jade. You down with that?" She hollered, then looked over her shoulder at me.

I was crouched in the corner of the boat trying to breathe. Every few minutes a strong, stabbing feeling coursed through me. It hurt so bad that tears were coming out of my eyes. "Bitch, I'll be ready." I gasped as water splashed up and landed on my face from the ocean. "I ain't ducking no action from you, Jazzy."

She cracked up. "You lucky I'm helping you, Jade. You the one broad that I hate with all of my might. Straight up. But the way I see it you ain't got shit else I can take from you. I already got yo nigga. That's all I wanted to begin with. Long as I got him, don't shit else matter. Our baby gon be way prettier than yours. When I pop this one out, he ain't gon think twice about that lil gremlin you carrying." She laughed and increased the speeds on the boat.

Baby? Was this her way of bragging about her being pregnant? Had Bentley screwed me over like that? I turned to look across the boat at him. He avoided eye contact. "Baby, Bentley? Seriously?"

He looked off and shook his head. What did that even mean? Was it his way of confirming that he knew? What was going on inside of his mind? He'd been quiet ever since we'd gotten in the boat.

"He ain't got nothing else to say to you, Jade. You made your decision. All you care about is those girls, so you about to get them and be on your way. Good riddance, bitch. Word up." Jazzy laughed, as the boat bouncing up and down on the water.

I felt another sharp pain shoot through me. This one took my breath completely away.

I closed my eyes and tried to control my breathing. Bentley came over and rubbed my back. I allowed for that to take place for a second and then I smacked his hands away. "Get off of me, you son of a bitch. I hate you!" I yelled in so much pain that I could barely see straight.

Jazzy looked over her shoulders and mugged him. He scooted back across the boat and looked out into the water. I didn't know what kind of a hold she had on him, but it was sickening to watch. My heart officially ripped down on the middle. I felt like breaking down. Somewhere along the way I'd lost my husband to a low-life, cutthroat woman. I didn't understand it, but I kept on hearing my mother's voice in my head telling me over and over again that men were evil. That all they cared about were themselves. Sooner or later, they always hurt you. That the actions of my father were a reflection of what all men were destined to become over time. That it was always good in the beginning. The beginning is when they are on their best behavior. I thought about all that me and Bentley had been through, all that we had overcome together, and I just could not believe that his loyalty to me could be so watered down. I was hurt to say the least. We were shattered. Now I had to focus on getting my sisters back, and my child. Clearly he had made his mind up and he'd chosen Jazzy. I curled into a ball on the floor of the boat and tried to breathe as easy as possible. Once again my eyes traveled over to Bentley. We made eye contact shortly, before he diverted his eyes and took a sip of the grape soda pop he was drinking on.

***

An hour later, the speed boat pulled into a dock that had two really big ships anchored. The dock was connected to a big orange packaging warehouse. The air smelled exactly like citrus. The sun continued to beam down on top of my head. The stale air was picking up humidity. Seagulls squawked overhead loudly. I allowed for Bentley to help me to get out of the boat and onto the dock as much as I didn't want him to. He draped my arm around his neck and placed his around my waist as we stepped off of the boat. "Come on, Jade. Hang in there. I got you. Just be careful," he said, helping me to make my way down the docks a few steps at a time. I caught string whiffs of his cologne and manly scent, and it made me reminisce a bit. Where had we went wrong? How had we fallen off of the path of us finding forever together? I never thought that we could be broken, yet here we were headed for two separate destinations.

I was sweating profusely. My legs trembled. Something wasn't right. I was beginning to feel sick. I needed to sit down. "Bentley, I need to sit down. I feel weak. It's too hot out here. Please let me sit down," I begged, becoming dizzy. I paused in place.

He stopped and looked me over. "Jade, you gotta keep going. You gotta make it to the twins. They need you. Come on." He tried to urge me along.

I felt a pain in my pelvic region. Then all of a sudden, my water broke. It created a big splash right between my legs. I buckled against Bentley and groaned.

Jazzy came and smacked me on the back of the head hard. "Keep it moving, Jade, if you want to see them lil girls again. If not, I can just stank yo ass and them too. I'm ready to be done with you anyway. Now move," she screamed.

Bentley helped me back up. "Come on Jade. The fruit ship is right there. We just gotta get you on there and it's a wrap. Just hold on, ma, please."

"How, Bentley? How am I going to do that? This baby is coming. It's coming and I can't stop it. I can't do this on my own." My knees got so weak that I nearly fell to the concrete, but Bentley caught me, and held me against him. Then I sank to the ground again.

"Jazzy, we gotta get her some help. She's about to go into labor. Help me with her," he hollered.

"You got me fucked up. Far as I'm concerned I'm doing enough for that Bitch. If it was up to me, I'd leave two in her dome, one in each of her sisters' heads and call it a day. Fuck I look like assisting this broad? Man, please. Let's go, Jade!"

I blew out a gust of air and willed myself to stand up. "Okay, come on, Bentley. Just help me meet our destination. Please! Argggh!" A contraction ripped through me. I clenched my teeth and hollered out in pain. Sweat beaded down my forehead and neck.

Bentley picked me up and carried me in his arms. He followed a laughing Jazzy into the big warehouse. Now that we were inside of it, the scent of oranges was ten times stronger. So much so that I could taste oranges on my tongue every time I inhaled. Though my vision was hazy, I could make out the interior of the warehouse. It was filled with a bunch of wooden crates. There were three forklifts,

166

a conveyer belt, and rows and rows of shelves with crates lining them.

Bentley set me down in the middle of the floor, knelt and wiped sweat from the side of my face. "Are you okay?"

I took quick breaths and ignored his ass, mugged him with hatred for getting us involved with this broad. I felt deep in my soul that things could not end well.

"Y'all stay right here. I'll be right back." She jogged over to one of the forklifts. Inserted a key and drove off with it beeping. She took one glance back at us and laughed.

Bentley continued to wipe at the side of my face. "Be strong, Jade. Please. Fight through the pain. You cannot have this baby right now."

I quickened my breaths. Another contraction ripped through me again. This one felt worse than the last one. I bit down on my lip until it bled, tightened my fist.

He kissed my forehead. "I got you, Jade. I just need for you to hold on for a little while longer. Your strength is everything right now. Just trust me."

I didn't. But once again, what other choice did I have? I was stuck between a rock and a hard place.

"How could you do this to me?" How could you leave me in the cold like this, Bentley? Ain't I gave you all of me?" I mustered. Tears ran down my eyes from the pain I was experiencing and the emotional abuse that he was taking me through. Everything came burrowing down on me at once.

"Please, Jade. Just bear with me. Just keep fighting, baby. We're so close. We can't be broken right now. You gotta know me better than this."

"I don't know you anymore, Bentley. I can't trust you. You've hurt me too much." I groaned, then doubled over. The pain was too intense.

There was a constant beeping of the forklift returning, the sound of the machine rolling across the floor. I forced myself to sit up. When I looked across the warehouse, I saw Jazzy balancing three big crates on the metal lifters of the forklift. She wasn't alone. It appeared that another woman was with her. She pulled the machine in front of me and Bentley and parked it, then slowly lowered the crates until they were on the ground. She hopped off of the forklift and walked over to Bentley, pulling him up. "Get the fuck away from that bitch, daddy. You're with me now. It's somebody I want you to meet." She took ahold of his hand and mugged me.

The other woman stepped off the forklift. She was short, about five feet even, dark-skinned, with a bald head. She was dressed in a tight black and green Prada dress that clung to her curves. She stepped up to us with her hand out. "Please to meet you, Bentley, I've heard nothing but good things."

He shook her hand and nodded. "I wish I could say the same. Who are you?"

"My name is Ruby, and I'm Jazzy's sister-in-law. I heard about all of the ways you've helped my husband, and I would like to return the favor. You see those big ships out there?

He nodded. "What about them?"

"Those ships are going to insure that this pregnant woman and those two little girls make it to Havana by morning. There is only one catch."

"What's that?" He looked down to Jazzy.

"First off, we're going to have to move fast and secondly, in order for this to work, she's going to have to get into this crate right here." Ruby tapped the crate that was on the very top twice. There was only enough room for three crates. These two already have her sisters in them. This one is for her."

"You put my fuckin' sisters in a crate! Bitch, I'ma kill you! Ahh!" Another contraction hit me so hard that I fell backward, the air taken out of me. It felt like the worst cramp I'd ever had times a million.

Jazzy bumped Ruby out of the way and pulled out a gun. She cocked it back. "I'm tired of this bitch's mouth. Tired of her threatening me." She grabbed a handful of my hair and pulled. This caused me to scream. I could feel the roots being yanked out of my scalp. "How about we kill you and that punk ass baby, Jade. How about that. Huh?"

I kicked my legs as she drug me across the floor. I was too weak to fight. I was in so much pain that I couldn't even think straight. "Stop. Stop. Bitch. Let me go!"

Bentley rushed over and took her hands out of my hair, pushed Jazzy so hard that she flew into the forklift and dropped her gun. "She pregnant, and in labor. What the fuck is wrong wit you, bitch?"

Her sister-in-law crept behind him and stuck a nine to the back of his head. "We don't allow for no nigga to put they hands on a female in the family. That shit a get you kilt, Haitian-style." She cocked the hammer.

Jazzy slowly got to her feet and pulled another gun from the small of her back. I scooted backward and fell on the first one she'd dropped, praying that it was a distant memory. She stepped up to Bentley and aimed the gun at his face. "You still love that bitch, don't you? You're choosing her over me?" She frowned.

Bentley swallowed his spit. "She pregnant, man. You just handling her a lil too rough Jazzy. That's all I'm saying. That wasn't a part of our agreement."

"Oh yeah, Bentley, well why don't you tell me what out agreement was then? What did we agree to, because right now I'm thinking fuck that agreement and we establish some new terms."

"I say we turn them in and get that two million. That's what I say," Ruby added.

"Shut up, bitch," Jazzy returned. "I run this shit. It's only one Queen B in this family and you ain't it. So fall back like dominos." She mugged Bentley. "What was the agreement?"

"That we was finna make sure that Jade, and the twins were able to sail away safe and sound. Once they were able to, then you and I would go our separate ways. A deal is a deal, Jazzy. We gotta honor that shit."

Jazzy pressed the barrel to his forehead and turned it sideways. "You think I'm stupid, don't you? You don't think I can tell you love that girl more than you do me? And all for what? She don't bring shit to the table? Why don't you love me, Bentley?" She pressed it harder into his skin. "Why?"

His head was all the way back. He clenched his jaw muscles. "I do love you."

My heart sank. I shouldn't have been hearing that. I couldn't believe he'd fallen for her. Where had I went wrong?"

"But it's just that the man in me needs to make sure that she's okay too. I can't explain it."

Jazzy laughed. "Yeah, right. As long as this bitch is walking the face of this earth, you're always going to love her more than me. And that's fucked up, because all she care about is these lil bitches in here. I'ma prove it." She stood to the side and kicked one of the crates.

170

Inside of it I could heard the sobbing of somebody crying. They beat on the box and screamed. I felt tears roll down my cheeks, and off of my chin.

"Jade! It's either your sister or Bentley. Where am I putting this first bullet? You got ten seconds. One. Two. Three. Four."

"No, don't do this, Jazzy. Please don't do this," I hollered.

"Five. Six. Seven. Eight. Speak up, Jade. Tell me. Tell me now!"

"Pop me! That's it, baby. I can handle it."

Jazzy shook her head. "N'all, fuck that." *Boom. Boom. Boom.*

The bullets crashed into the wood and knocked big holes inside of the box. The screaming stopped. There was an eerie silence in the room.

"Nooooooo!" I screamed.

Jazzy busted up laughing. "Now shit is about to get real. There is one more box left. Where are these bullets going, Jade? Are they going into your sister, or are they going into Bentley? You got another ten seconds. I wonder why that other bitch ain't making no noise. Wait a minute." She turned her gun around and beat on the box with the handle. Placed her ear to the side of it. "Hey, you okay in there?" There was more silence, and then a muffled sobbing. This brought a smile to Jazzy's face. She stepped back and aimed her gun at the crate. "Where is it going Jade? Tell me now."

"Jazzy, listen to me. Shoot me and get this shit over with. You're killing a child. What the fuck is wrong wit you? They are innocent."

She bucked her eyes. "They wouldn't be for long, Bentley. Sooner or later, somebody would get ahold of them. When they do, they're going to ruin them for all of eternity. It's just the way the world works. So in all honesty, I'm doing them a favor. Girls don't stand a chance in this world. Now where are these bullets going, Jade?" she screamed at the top of her lungs.

"I said in me. Put 'em in me. Please," Bentley said for the third time, but Jazzy appeared to purposely ignore him. As if she'd already had her mind made up. She was dead set on causing me as much pain as possible, before she turned the gun on me. At least, that's how I felt.

"Shoot me, Jazzy. I can't take this pain no more," I said, straining to even speak.

She bucked her eyes, then slowly began to smile, as she aimed the gun at me. "Bitch, with pleasure."

"Jazzy, nooooooo!" Bentley hollered, ran and jumped just as Jazzy's gun popped twice.

Chapter 19
Bentley

Boom. Boom.

I felt the bullets burn holes into my chest. I fell on top of Jade, covering her. It felt like I'd been poked in the chest two times by a flaming sword. I could feel them penetrate the bulletproof vest, lodging themselves into my body, and it hurt so bad that all I could do was keep my eyes closed tight.

"Bentley! Oh my God, baby! Why would you do that?" Jazzy screamed. She rushed over to me and tried to pull me off of Jade. But, I wasn't going. With the little bit of strength that I had left, I kept her covered with my body.

She shook under me. "Bentley. Bentley. Hubby. Say something, please," Jade begged.

I tried to move in the slightest and the pain intensified. "I'm good." My voice was raspy. Strained.

"That's it. I knew it. I knew it, Bentley. You're still in love with this bitch. You love her so much that you're willing to die for her! Nobody would ever do that for me, and it's not fair. It's not fair!" From the corners of my eyes I saw her raise both guns. She aimed them down at me with tears coming down her eyes. "I could have loved you with all that I was, Bentley. Me and you could have changed the world. But that's okay. I should have known you never be mine. Ruby, there are two suitcases around the corner right on the floor by those empty crates. Grab them, and come back here."

"Alright, sis." Ruby jogged off to follow her orders.

Jazzy kept her pistols trained on me. "You want her so bad? You gonna die with this bitch then. Move, Bentley! Get the fuck out of the way! I'm about to shoot. I swear on my mother, I am. You got five seconds. One, two..."

I covered my head and made sure that my entire body was over Jade, prepared to feel the barrage of bullets that were sure to come. It was a fucked-up demise, but as long as I died beside the love of my life, everything that we had been through had been worth this moment.

"Kill them!" Ruby hollered as she returned, carrying the two suitcases.

"Get off of me, Bentley!" Jade wiggled up under me. "Get the fuck off of me." She stuck her thumb into one of the bullet holes inside of my chest. The pain was so unbearable that I hollered out in agony.

"Argh!" I fell to the side of her, leaving my pregnant wife exposed. After the initial shock I struggled to get back on top of her.

But she scooted away on her backside, and laid down on her back and screamed, "Hey, Jazzy! You punk bitch!"

Jazzy looked over to her, with eyes wide open. Her guns were still aimed down at me. But something about Jade made her struggle to angle her guns that way.

"Jazzy, watch out!" Ruby yelled and dove to the floor, throwing the suitcases to each side of her.

Boom. Boom. Boom. Boom. Boom. Boom. Boom.

The gun jumped in Jade's hand again and again. Jade's bullets stood Jazzy straight up. Hole after hole filled her body. She flew backward into the forklift, and slowly slid to her knees with her eyes open as big as flashlights. Dropped her gun, and fell face first on the concrete, blood pouring out of her.

"Don't you move either, bitch. Aw. Fuck. Stand up," Jade ordered, standing up herself and holding her stomach. Water and what looked like traces of blood sliding down her ankle out of her jeans. She cringed with each step she took toward Ruby.

174

Ruby held her hands up. "Please don't kill me. I ain't have nothing to do with that shit. I swear." She stood up and kept her hands in the air. Walking backward until she wound up bumping into one of the forklifts.

I rolled to my side, and slowly on to my ass, scooted backward with the throbbing pain inside of my chest. Sweat drenched my face and back. My breathing was rugged. Every time I swallowed it hurt and felt like I was being stabbed in the chest with a dull butter knife.

Jade got over to her, and screamed from the pain she was experiencing with her contractions, I surmised. Held the gun out. "Bitch, where is that gun you had?"

"What gun?" Ruby asked, playing dumb.

"The gun you stuck to the back of my husband's head. That gun?" Jade yelled, shaking her gun.

"It's in my lower back. Take it. I swear to God, I don't want no beef with you. Please. I'll help you get out of this country. That's all I was supposed to do anyway."

Jade held the gun pointed at her face, and reached around her body. Came up with the nine millimeter Beretta that she carried. Took her first gun and placed it on her waist. "You damn right you gon help us get out of here. We're boarding one of those ships out there, and you're going to tell me the procedure. Aren't you, Ruby?"

"Yes!"

"Good. Now what's in those suitcases?" Jade asked. She stopped and doubled over. "Aw! Fuck!" Fell to her knees with her eyes closed.

Ruby punched her in the face and jumped on top of her. They began to wrestle with the gun. Grunting and groaning.

Boom. The gun spit a round toward the ceiling of the warehouse. Seconds later, it fired again. *Boom.* They continued to tussle.

I low crawled across the floor. Dizzy. Blood leaking out of me, I felt as if I were being drained, my energy non-existent. I had to will my way toward them.

Jade hollered out again. "Help, Bentley. This bitch is strong!"

I got to my knees and rushed as fast as I could. Feeling like I was on the verge of an asthma attack, my breath becoming shorter and shorter. When I got close enough, I leaped and tackled Ruby off of Jade. Fell to the ground with her in a Full Nelson. Then my arm was around her neck, choking, pulling upward.

She gagged and kicked her feet. Scratched at my arm. Dug her nails into my arm. I tightened my hold and tried to not think about the liquid oozing out of my chest. Made my hold as tight as I could and locked it in until she stopped struggling underneath me, only then did I release her and fall back.

Jade lay on her back breathing hard. "Bentley. This baby is coming now. It's coming Bentley! Oh my God, it's coming!" She took deep breaths. "Help me!"

I rushed to her and unbuttoned her pants. Pulled them down her ankles and off. Cast them aside, and then her panties. Her Kitty was opened wider than I had ever seen it. It caught me off guard at first. Then I got ahold of myself. "Breathe, baby. Breathe. Come on, you can do this." I encouraged, losing her thighs as wide as they could go and placing her ankles on my shoulders.

"Bentley! Bentley! It hurt so bad! It hurt so bad! Uh! Uh!"

"Push baby! Push!"

She screamed and pushed as hard as she could. Closed her eyes and puffed up her jaws. Sweat peppered her forehead. Her neck was wet with it as well.

I stuck my head between her legs and saw our child crowning. I could see the wavy hair. The sight freaked me out and helped me to become excited at the same time. For the moment I forgot about the incessant pains in my chest. "Push baby. I see it. I see it, Jade. It's almost here."

"Okay. Okay." She nodded and blew out a gasp of air again. "Awwww!" She hollered and grabbed her ankles. Pushing with everything that she had.

The baby's head eased past her lips and popped out into the world. It's beautiful face fully visible. "Holy crap. It's here. It's here, Jade. Keep pushing."

She did.

Now there was a neck. Then shoulders. A chest. Stomach. The rest of the body slipped out, attached to an umbilical cord. I hurried and took my shirt off. Folded it and set the baby on it. Cleared its mouth and smacked the bottom. This made it cry. I halfway swaddled the baby inside of the shirt. Unable to do it fully because of the umbilical cord. "How do I cut it baby. What do I use?"

"Your knife, Bentley. Use that little Swiss Army thing that you carry."

I removed it from my pocket and opened it up. Balancing our screaming child in my arms, I flipped open the knife portion of it and sawed into the umbilical cord, cutting it.

Jade laid back and breathed a sigh of relief. "What is it, Bentley? What did we have?" she asked wearily.

In my haste to deliver our child I had not even paid attention. I removed enough of the shirt so I could see the sex of our baby. When I saw it, I smiled. "Baby, it's a. It's a..." My eyes crossed and everything went black.

***

Havana, Cuba
Six months later...
Jade

"You gotta pull on the rope harder than that, Bentley. Come on, put some muscle into it," I teased, as I sat back in my seat on the small boat.

A shirtless Bentley pulled on the cord as hard as he could, then tied it around the hook to make our sail spread out as far as possible. "Baby, it ain't gon get no better than that. Dang. I'm getting all kinds of rope burn." He frowned. Finished his job, before taking a seat beside me. "Besides, we should be paying somebody to do this for us. What's the use of having all of this money if we can't have a bunch of workers?" He said this taking our son Ashton from my arms. Ashton was his spitting image. It amazed me how much they actually looked alike.

"Because, we're supposed to be keeping a low profile. This is our new life we have to be careful with it. There is nothing that a worker can do that you can't do. Boy please." I rolled my eyes and laughed.

Ashland came over and sat beside me, typing away on her I-pad. For some reason she'd become obsessed with the game Fortnite. She even took to doing the dances that were on the game. "Yes!" She exclaimed pumping her fist in the air. "Level ten."

"Okay then lil mama," Bentley said, giving her a high five.

Ashley, rolled her eyes and smacked her lips. She was playing a different game in her I-pad. "Still not getting it Ashland. That game is for boys."

"Nun-uh. Is it Jade?" Ashland asked, looking over at me for clarification.

178

I looked over the scar tissue on her shoulder from where Jazzy's bullet had grazed her, and was so happy that my sister was alive. I couldn't help but to smile. "It's for anyone that wants to play and conquer it. Ashton, stop being so mean."

She sighed. "I'm sorry."

Bentley placed his arm around my shoulder. Leaned down and kissed Ashton. "It's just me and you son. We gotta make sure these ladies don't drive us crazy." He picked him up and kissed his chubby cheeks. Ashton smiled. His deep dimples were prominent. His father's young twin.

After Bentley had passed out, two of the Spanish men that worked on the biggest orange ship showed up at the warehouse, and saw what had taken place, and at the promise of fifty grand a piece decided to help us to board their ship after they uncovered the twins from their crates and revealed the fact that Ashland had only been grazed by Jazzy's bullets. Thank God for that. The hid us in the deck of their boat until the ship docked in Havana. Once there, we were rushed to the hospital where the staff worked on each of us with tender love and care. I gave birth to a healthy baby boy of six pounds and eleven ounces. I was so moved by their generosity that out of the two million dollars that Jazzy had left behind, I gave them an additional fifty grand, and the rest is history.

We bought ourselves a nice home, and here we are six months later in the deepest form of love that I've ever known. Bentley finds ways every single day to let me know that I am special, and that he appreciates me. He's a bit more overprotective, but who wouldn't be after all we've been through. He is the love of my life and more than I could have ever asked for. We remain in our Bibles, and every single day we struggle to get closer to Jehovah.

Our past is the past, but I know that we have many demons that are lurking to seek their revenge for the many wrongs we've done. I continue to pray about that, and it's all I can do.

The bounty for our arrests had skyrocketed to five million apiece after the warehouse debacle. I guess it's safe to say that we won't be going anywhere near the United States anytime soon.

"Baby, look." Bentley pointed.

Ashland and Ashley stood beside one another with their arms behind their backs. In unison they came from behind them holding out a jewelry boxes in front of them. "Because you're a true queen and we love you Jade." They opened them at the same time and looked over to Bentley.

Inside of the boxes were a necklace laced with pink diamonds and a matching diamond tennis bracelet that sparkled in the sun.

He smiled, his deep dimples causing me to shudder. "Damn baby, ain't you gon say somethin? That's pink lemonade diamonds right there girl." He continued to bounce Ashton up and down, patting his pamper.

I shook my head and laid back in the small lounge chair. "So, this is what it feels like to be treated like a Queen, huh?"

God was so good.

THE END

We just wanted to take the time out to say thank you to our readers. We appreciate the continued support; for every purchase, every share, every download, every review, etc. We do not take you all for granted. Loyal supporters are hard to come by and we are forever grateful. God has given us this gift to tell a story, and we pray that He continues to help us grow and to continue to help touch the lives of others. Stay blessed.

Love Always,

T.J. & Jelissa
#TheDreamTeam

Submission Guideline

Submit the first three chapters of your completed manuscript to ldpsubmissions@gmail.com, subject line: Your book's title. The manuscript must be in a .doc file and sent as an attachment. Document should be in Times New Roman, double spaced and in size 12 font. Also, provide your synopsis and full contact information. If sending multiple submissions, they must each be in a separate email.

Have a story but no way to send it electronically? You can still submit to LDP/Ca$h Presents. Send in the first three chapters, written or typed, of your completed manuscript to:

**LDP: Submissions Dept
Po Box 870494
Mesquite, Tx 75187**

DO NOT send original manuscript. Must be a duplicate.

Provide your synopsis and a cover letter containing your full contact information.

Thanks for considering LDP and Ca$h Presents.

Coming Soon from Lock Down Publications/Ca$h Presents

BOW DOWN TO MY GANGSTA

By **Ca$h**

TORN BETWEEN TWO

By **Coffee**

BLOOD STAINS OF A SHOTTA **III**

By **Jamaica**

STEADY MOBBIN **III**

By **Marcellus Allen**

RENEGADE BOYS IV

By Meesha

BLOOD OF A BOSS **VI**

SHADOWS OF THE GAME II

By **Askari**

LOYAL TO THE GAME **IV**

By **T.J. & Jelissa**

A DOPEBOY'S PRAYER **II**

By **Eddie "Wolf" Lee**

IF LOVING YOU IS WRONG… **III**

By **Jelissa**

TRUE SAVAGE **VII**

By **Chris Green**

BLAST FOR ME **III**

DUFFLE BAG CARTEL **IV**

HEARTLESS GOON **II**

By **Ghost**

T.J. & Jelissa

A HUSTLER'S DECEIT III

KILL ZONE **II**

BAE BELONGS TO ME III

SOUL OF A MONSTER III

By **Aryanna**

THE COST OF LOYALTY **III**

By **Kweli**

A GANGSTER'S SYN III

THE SAVAGE LIFE II

By **J-Blunt**

KING OF NEW YORK V

RISE TO POWER III

COKE KINGS IV

BORN HEARTLESS II

By **T.J. Edwards**

GORILLAZ IN THE BAY IV

De'Kari

THE STREETS ARE CALLING II

Duquie Wilson

KINGPIN KILLAZ IV

STREET KINGS III

PAID IN BLOOD III

CARTEL KILLAZ II

Hood Rich

SINS OF A HUSTLA II

ASAD

TRIGGADALE III

Elijah R. Freeman

KINGZ OF THE GAME IV

Playa Ray

SLAUGHTER GANG IV

RUTHLESS HEART II

By Willie Slaughter

THE HEART OF A SAVAGE II

By Jibril Williams

FUK SHYT II

By Blakk Diamond

THE DOPEMAN'S BODYGAURD II

By Tranay Adams

TRAP GOD II

By Troublesome

YAYO II

By S. Allen

GHOST MOB

Stilloan Robinson

KINGPIN DREAMS

By Paper Boi Rari

CREAM

By Yolanda Moore

SON OF A DOPE FIEND II

By Renta

Available Now

RESTRAINING ORDER **I & II**

By **CA$H & Coffee**

LOVE KNOWS NO BOUNDARIES **I II & III**

By **Coffee**

RAISED AS A GOON I, II, III & IV

BRED BY THE SLUMS I, II, III

BLAST FOR ME I & II

ROTTEN TO THE CORE I II III

A BRONX TALE I, II, III

DUFFEL BAG CARTEL I II III

HEARTLESS GOON

A SAVAGE DOPEBOY

HEARTLESS GOON

By **Ghost**

LAY IT DOWN **I & II**

LAST OF A DYING BREED

BLOOD STAINS OF A SHOTTA I & II

By **Jamaica**

LOYAL TO THE GAME

LOYAL TO THE GAME II

LOYAL TO THE GAME III

LIFE OF SIN I, II III

By **TJ & Jelissa**

BLOODY COMMAS I & II

SKI MASK CARTEL I II & III

KING OF NEW YORK I II,III IV

RISE TO POWER I II

COKE KINGS I II III

BORN HEARTLESS

By **T.J. Edwards**

IF LOVING HIM IS WRONG…I & II

LOVE ME EVEN WHEN IT HURTS I II III

By **Jelissa**

WHEN THE STREETS CLAP BACK I & II III

By **Jibril Williams**

A DISTINGUISHED THUG STOLE MY HEART I II & III

LOVE SHOULDN'T HURT I II III IV

RENEGADE BOYS I II III

By **Meesha**

A GANGSTER'S CODE I &, II III

A GANGSTER'S SYN I II

THE SAVAGE LIFE

By **J-Blunt**

PUSH IT TO THE LIMIT

By **Bre' Hayes**

BLOOD OF A BOSS **I, II, III, IV, V**

SHADOWS OF THE GAME

By **Askari**

THE STREETS BLEED MURDER **I, II & III**

THE HEART OF A GANGSTA I II& III

By **Jerry Jackson**

CUM FOR ME

CUM FOR ME 2

CUM FOR ME 3

CUM FOR ME 4

CUM FOR ME 5

An **LDP Erotica Collaboration**

BRIDE OF A HUSTLA **I II & II**

THE FETTI GIRLS **I, II& III**

CORRUPTED BY A GANGSTA I, II III, IV

BLINDED BY HIS LOVE

By **Destiny Skai**

WHEN A GOOD GIRL GOES BAD

By **Adrienne**

THE COST OF LOYALTY I II

By Kweli

A GANGSTER'S REVENGE **I II III & IV**

THE BOSS MAN'S DAUGHTERS

THE BOSS MAN'S DAUGHTERS II

THE BOSSMAN'S DAUGHTERS III

THE BOSSMAN'S DAUGHTERS IV

THE BOSS MAN'S DAUGHTERS **V**

A SAVAGE LOVE **I & II**

BAE BELONGS TO ME I II

A HUSTLER'S DECEIT I, II, III

WHAT BAD BITCHES DO I, II, III

SOUL OF A MONSTER I II

KILL ZONE

By **Aryanna**

A KINGPIN'S AMBITON

A KINGPIN'S AMBITION **II**

I MURDER FOR THE DOUGH

By **Ambitious**

TRUE SAVAGE

TRUE SAVAGE II

TRUE SAVAGE **III**

TRUE SAVAGE **IV**

TRUE SAVAGE **V**

TRUE SAVAGE **VI**

By **Chris Green**

A DOPEBOY'S PRAYER

By **Eddie "Wolf" Lee**

THE KING CARTEL **I, II & III**

By **Frank Gresham**

THESE NIGGAS AIN'T LOYAL **I, II & III**

By **Nikki Tee**

GANGSTA SHYT **I II &III**

By **CATO**

THE ULTIMATE BETRAYAL

By **Phoenix**

BOSS'N UP **I , II & III**

By **Royal Nicole**

I LOVE YOU TO DEATH

By Destiny J

I RIDE FOR MY HITTA

I STILL RIDE FOR MY HITTA

T.J. & Jelissa

By **Misty Holt**

LOVE & CHASIN' PAPER

By **Qay Crockett**

TO DIE IN VAIN

SINS OF A HUSTLA

By **ASAD**

BROOKLYN HUSTLAZ

By **Boogsy Morina**

BROOKLYN ON LOCK I & II

By **Sonovia**

GANGSTA CITY

By **Teddy Duke**

A DRUG KING AND HIS DIAMOND I & II III

A DOPEMAN'S RICHES

HER MAN, MINE'S TOO I, II

CASH MONEY HO'S

By Nicole Goosby

TRAPHOUSE KING **I II & III**

KINGPIN KILLAZ I II III

STREET KINGS I II

PAID IN BLOOD **I II**

CARTEL KILLAZ

By **Hood Rich**

LIPSTICK KILLAH **I, II, III**

CRIME OF PASSION I & II

By **Mimi**

STEADY MOBBN' **I, II, III**

Life of Sin 3

By **Marcellus Allen**

WHO SHOT YA **I, II, III**

SON OF A DOPE FIEND

Renta

GORILLAZ IN THE BAY **I II III**

DE'KARI

TRIGGADALE I II

Elijah R. Freeman

GOD BLESS THE TRAPPERS I, II, III

THESE SCANDALOUS STREETS I, II, III

FEAR MY GANGSTA I, II, III

THESE STREETS DON'T LOVE NOBODY I, II

BURY ME A G I, II, III, IV, V

A GANGSTA'S EMPIRE I, II, III, IV

THE DOPEMAN'S BODYGAURD

Tranay Adams

THE STREETS ARE CALLING

Duquie Wilson

MARRIED TO A BOSS… I II III

By Destiny Skai & Chris Green

KINGZ OF THE GAME I II III

Playa Ray

SLAUGHTER GANG I II III

RUTHLESS HEART

By Willie Slaughter

THE HEART OF A SAVAGE

By Jibril Williams

FUK SHYT

By Blakk Diamond

DON'T F#CK WITH MY HEART I II

By Linnea

ADDICTED TO THE DRAMA I II III

By Jamila

YAYO

By S. Allen

TRAP GOD

By Troublesome

BOOKS BY LDP'S CEO, CA$H

TRUST IN NO MAN

TRUST IN NO MAN 2

TRUST IN NO MAN 3

BONDED BY BLOOD

SHORTY GOT A THUG

THUGS CRY

THUGS CRY 2

THUGS CRY 3

TRUST NO BITCH

TRUST NO BITCH 2

TRUST NO BITCH 3

TIL MY CASKET DROPS

RESTRAINING ORDER

RESTRAINING ORDER 2

IN LOVE WITH A CONVICT

Coming Soon

BONDED BY BLOOD 2

BOW DOWN TO MY GANGSTA

T.J. & Jelissa